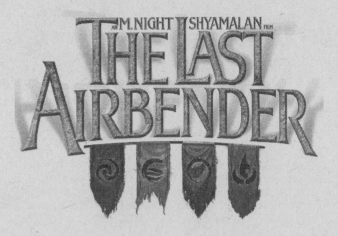

AN M. NIGHT SHYAMALAN FILM

THE LAST AIRBENDER

MOVIE NOVELIZATION

D0168511

adapted by Michael Teitelbaum
based on the series *Avatar: The Last Airbender* created by
Michael Dante DiMartino and Bryan Konietzko
based on the screenplay written by M. Night Shyamalan

Simon Spotlight
New York   London   Toronto   Sydney

SIMON SPOTLIGHT
An imprint of Simon & Schuster Children's Publishing Division
1230 Avenue of the Americas, New York, New York 10020.
© 2010 by Paramount Pictures. All Rights Reserved. The Last Airbender, The Last Airbender and all related titles, logos and characters are trademarks of Viacom International Inc. All rights reserved, including the right of reproduction in whole or in part in any form. SIMON SPOTLIGHT and colophon are registered trademarks of Simon & Schuster, Inc.
For information about special discounts for bulk purchases, please contact Simon & Schuster Special Sales at 1-866-506-1949 or business@simonandschuster.com.
Manufactured in the United States of America 0410 OFF
First Edition 10 9 8 7 6 5 4 3 2 1   ISBN 978-1-4424-0174-7

PROLOGUE

Water. Earth. Fire. Air. Each element defines a great nation. My grandmother used to tell me stories about the old days, about a time of peace when the Avatar kept balance among the four nations: the Water Tribes, the Earth Kingdom, the Fire Nation, and the Air Nomads.

But all that changed when the comet came.

It blazed across the sky and gave the firebenders a moment of great power. And during that moment, the Fire Nation attacked. They started a terrible war—a war that continues to this day.

Only the Avatar, master of all four elements and the bridge to the spirit world, could stop the ruthless firebenders. But when the world needed him most, he vanished.

One hundred years have passed since the Avatar

disappeared. The Fire Nation has learned to make metal machines of war, and they are nearing victory.

My name is Katara. I am a waterbender from the Southern Water Tribe. Two years ago my father and the other men of my tribe journeyed to the Earth Kingdom to help fight against the Fire Nation. My father left me and my brother to look after our tribe. Most people believe that the Avatar was never reborn into the Air Nomads as was supposed to happen and that the cycle of the Avatar has been broken forever. But I haven't lost hope.

I still believe that somehow the Avatar will return to save the world!

CHAPTER 1

Sunlight glinted off an endless expanse of ice dotted with towering glaciers of white. Cutting through the frozen plain, a river wended its way, twisting and flowing, creating movement in the otherwise still landscape.

A small paddle boat carrying two passengers drifted to shore. A seventeen-year-old boy hopped out and bent down to tie the craft to a piece of ice that jutted out of the frozen shore. A fifteen-year-old girl who had been seated beside him climbed out and stood at the water's edge.

She held her hands over the rushing river and began to concentrate. Thoughts of all that had happened to her and her people flooded her mind. One image appeared and crowded out all the others; it was the kind face of her mother. She felt a rush of warmth and love, though it was tinged with anger and sadness.

Focusing on the positive feelings, the girl rotated and lifted her hands. A small amount of water bubbled, then rose from the river and hovered in the air in front of her. Flexing her fingers, she rounded the water into the shape of a sphere. When the girl turned and stepped away from the river's edge, the water moved with her, as if she were carrying it in an invisible container.

She turned toward the boy, and the ball of water followed her movement. It now hovered directly above his head. Taking a step forward, the girl stumbled on the uneven ice. As she moved her hands to regain her balance, she lost control of the water, which came splashing down onto the boy's head.

"I'm sorry, Sokka," the girl cried, unable to hold back a small giggle as he tried to chase his sister around on the ice.

"I thought about Mom that time," the girl said, changing direction to stay a few steps ahead of him. "And it worked better. Isn't that strange?"

"Yeah, I guess so, Katara," the boy grumbled, slowing down. "Whatever. Just stop doing that water stuff around me. It always ends up with me getting wet."

"It's called waterbending," Katara said, coming to a stop.

"I know what it's called," Sokka shot back. "Just quit doing it over my head!"

Reaching back into the boat, Sokka pulled out a spear. He stepped quietly around the edge of an ice mountain, gripping the weapon tightly. Katara followed a few steps behind.

Sokka spotted something in the ice just ahead. Kneeling down, he ran his hand along the edge of a series of tracks in the dusting of snow that covered the ice.

"It's a tigerseal," he said to his sister.

"Are you sure?" Katara asked.

Sokka nodded, then he quickly started to follow the tracks. Katara hurried to keep up with her brother.

A few minutes later they stepped through a narrow gap between two glaciers and stared at a vast field of ice—flat, featureless, and eerily quiet.

"Uh, Sokka, are we lost?" Katara asked, looking out at the endless stretch of nothingness.

"I did everything Dad said to do," Sokka replied. He was frustrated, but not ready to admit that the two were lost. "There's no way we should be—"

"Sokka, wait!" Katara said, grabbing her brother's arm.

"What is it, Katara?" Sokka asked, sensing her tension.

Katara pointed down at the ice. A white glow radiated up from deep below the surface. Sokka looked down and immediately reached into his backpack, pulling out a boomerang. Kneeling, he peered into the glowing ice.

"Something's under there," he said.

He raised his boomerang and slammed its edge down onto the ice. Nothing happened. He whacked the ice again. Still nothing. Striking the ice for the third time, Sokka heard an unmistakable cracking sound.

The ice beneath his feet began to spiderweb in every direction. The cracks grew longer and wider, opening gaping holes in the ice.

"It's a cave-in!" he shouted to Katara. "Move away from the cracks!"

The two backed away and watched from a safe distance as a huge ball of ice rose from under the surface and emerged from a large opening. The smooth, clear sphere finally stopped moving. The ice plain grew silent once again.

Katara stepped forward.

"We shouldn't touch it," Sokka said anxiously.

"But look," Katara insisted, pointing. "There's someone in there. It looks like a boy. Who is he? Is he alive?"

"This could be a Fire Nation trap," Sokka pointed out, slipping his boomerang into his pack and grabbing Katara's hand. "Let's get back to the village."

"We can't just leave him, Sokka!" Katara cried.

Sokka shrugged. "He's probably dead, anyway."

Katara snatched the boomerang from her brother's pack and ran toward the giant ice ball.

"Wait, don't!" Sokka cried.

Ignoring her brother, Katara smacked the huge ball of ice with the edge of the boomerang.

"There could be a lot of built-up pressure inside that thing," Sokka insisted.

Katara struck the sphere again.

Sokka sighed deeply and shook his head. Since when did his sister ever listen to him, anyway?

"Katara, you don't know what might—"

A powerful blast of air shot from a crack in the sphere, blowing Katara back and across the ice. She slammed into Sokka, and the two skidded to a stop.

"—happen," Sokka finished as he untangled himself from his sister.

The crack Katara had opened expanded, and a blinding light shot high into the sky, turning the whole world white. Sokka and Katara shielded their eyes, trying in vain to see what was going on.

The light faded, revealing that the sphere had split in half, leaving two motionless figures sprawled out on the ice. The boy Katara had seen inside it was wrapped in a cloak. Beside him lay a huge animal covered in thick white fur.

Katara kneeled down next to the boy, who appeared to be about thirteen years old. His head was shaved completely bald and covered by a blue tattoo in the shape of an arrow. Katara leaned in close just as the boy opened his eyes.

"Is he breathing?" Sokka asked. "And did you see that light shoot into the sky? What was that all about?"

Katara smiled at the boy. "What's your name?" she asked softly.

The boy squinted up at her but remained silent.

"He's exhausted, Sokka," Katara said, realizing that this was no place for a conversation. "We need to get him back to the village."

Sokka walked up to the big furry creature and started poking the beast. "What is this thing?" he wondered aloud.

The enormous animal casually lifted his huge, paddle-like tail and pinned Sokka beneath it.

"Help!" he cried, flailing his arms from underneath the tail. "I'm being attacked!"

Katara stood and spun around quickly, wondering how she could possibly battle this enormous beast. Then Sokka easily crawled out from under the tail. The animal made no attempt to stop him.

"False alarm," Sokka said, standing up and brushing the ice and white fur from his jacket. "Everything's under control."

Katara turned back to the boy and helped him to his feet. "Hold my hand," she said gently. "You'll be okay."

The boy fell into her arms, unconscious. "Sokka, help me get him back to the boat," she said.

They retraced their steps and carried the unconscious boy back to their boat. Sokka paddled quickly down the river toward their village. Glancing over his shoulder, he noticed the big white animal following them along the shoreline.

A short time later they arrived at their village, a small collection of igloos nestled together at the bottom of an ice valley. Carrying the boy, they brought him to their grandmother's igloo. She helped them bring the boy inside and get him comfortably settled.

As their grandmother attended to the boy, Sokka ran off to check on the tribe's children. This was one of the responsibilities his father had left him with when he went off with the other men of the tribe to fight against the Fire Nation.

"He's all right," Katara's grandmother said when Sokka returned. She signaled for them to step outside. "He just needs some rest." Katara and Sokka stepped out of the igloo, and the older woman looked at her granddaughter.

"Where exactly did you find him, Katara?" she asked.

"By a path near the big glaciers," Katara replied. "He was buried in the ice."

Her grandmother turned away, her wrinkled, weather-beaten face creased in thought.

"What's wrong, Grandma?" Katara asked, wondering if saving the boy could have possibly been the wrong thing to do.

Grandma's expression softened. "Nothing's wrong, Katara," she said. "Go keep an eye on the boy, so he is not alone when he awakens."

Katara nodded and slipped back into the igloo. To her surprise the boy was awake, standing up and putting on his shirt. She stared in amazement at the intricate pattern of tattoos that ran down from his head and across his back and arms. His body was thin but muscular. When the boy had put on his shirt and cloak, he noticed Katara.

"How did you get all the way out here?" she asked. "This village is pretty far away from the rest of the world."

"I ran away from home," the boy stated flatly. "It wasn't a very smart thing to do. I was just upset."

Katara thought about all she had faced since the war began and how many times she wished that she could have simply run away. "I get like that too," she said.

"Thanks for saving me," the boy said, smiling for the first time.

"Just lucky," Katara admitted.

The boy sighed deeply. "I probably should get home," he said, wrapping his cloak around him. "They'll all be worried."

"So you're going home?" Katara asked. "Then you're not still upset?"

"Not as much as I was," the boy explained, picking up a wooden staff that was as tall as he was. He noticed Katara fidgeting with the necklace that hung around her neck.

Katara blushed as the boy reached out and touched the carved wooden necklace. "It's my mom's," she said softly. "She gave it to me."

"You're lucky to have family," the cloaked boy said with a touch of sadness in his voice.

"She passed away," Katara said.

"Oh, sorry," the boy said, feeling uncomfortable.

"But you're right," Katara added quickly. "I *was* lucky."

The boy nodded, then suddenly seemed worried.

"Your animal—," Katara began.

"Appa is his name," the boy explained.

"You don't have to worry," she continued. "He's just at the edge of the village, near the stream. He's fine. He's very gentle."

"I should go," the boy said. "I—"

Just then, Sokka rushed into the igloo, leading a group of village children. His face was flushed, and his eyes were wide with fear.

"The Fire Nation's here," he said tersely. "And they brought their war machines."

CHAPTER 2

Sokka got the children settled inside his grandmother's igloo. "Don't come out until I tell you it's safe," he said sternly. The children all nodded and huddled together anxiously.

"Is something wrong?" the cloaked boy asked. "Should I come?"

"No," Katara replied quickly. "Please wait here."

As Sokka and Katara stepped toward the igloo doorway, Katara looked back at the mysterious boy.

Leaning his tall staff against the wall, he turned to the frightened group of children. "Don't worry," he said, smiling. "I'm sure there's nothing wrong." He pulled a handful of stones from the pocket of his cloak. "Who wants to play a game?" he asked.

The children gathered around the boy, who kneeled

down and tossed the stones onto the floor.

Katara turned and joined her brother outside. They were terrified to see massive Fire Nation metal warships docked at the edge of the village.

Fire Nation soldiers marched off the ships and through the village. Some villagers bowed respectfully. Others cowered in fear. Sokka and Katara paused as the group of soldiers approached.

"It can't be a coincidence that we break that kid out of the ice and light shoots into the sky and now the Fire Nation is here," Sokka said anxiously.

As the line of marching soldiers reached him, Sokka's hand moved slowly to his boomerang. He gripped it tightly.

"Sokka, don't," Katara whispered urgently.

Sokka fought back his anger and the urge to strike out at these soldiers. He thought of the pain and destruction they had already brought down on his family, his people, and the whole world.

The soldier at the front of the platoon pulled off his helmet, revealing a youthful yet hardened face. A burn scar ran along the left side of his face.

"I am Prince Zuko, son of Fire Lord Ozai and heir to the throne of the Fire Nation," the young soldier announced to the frightened villagers. "Bring me all your elderly."

None of the villagers moved, so the Fire Nation soldiers went from igloo to igloo, pulling the eldest members of the tribe out of their homes.

When a Fire Nation soldier arrived with Sokka and Katara's grandmother, Katara's face stiffened. She opened her hands and focused her mind. A small snowdrift near her feet began to swirl into a funnel shape. The mini-tornado rose toward her hands.

Sokka glanced down and noticed the rising snow. "Katara, don't," he whispered. His sister allowed the snow to fall harmlessly back to the ground.

Back in the igloo, a child tossed a stone into a group of other stones that were placed in a circle. The other children near him all cheered.

"You're good at that," said the cloaked boy, who was leading the game. "Now I'll show you one of my favorite games."

A shadow fell over him as a Fire Nation soldier stepped into the igloo. He stared at the boy for a moment, then pulled off his cloak revealing the arrow-shaped tattoo running across his head. He grabbed the boy and pulled him outside as the children huddled together in fear.

Back outside Katara leaned close to her brother. "What do they want with the elders?" she whispered.

Before Sokka could reply, the soldier pulled the tattooed boy and shoved him in front of Prince Zuko. Katara's eyes opened wide.

"You're scaring these people," the cloaked boy said firmly.

"That's the point," Prince Zuko replied. He stared at the strange-looking boy. "Who are you? What's your name?"

"I don't need to tell you anything," the boy snarled defiantly, staring right at Zuko.

The prince turned to his troops. "Firebenders!" he shouted. A group of soldiers stepped forward and immediately surrounded the boy. Then Prince Zuko pointed at his metal warship. "I'm taking you to my ship. And if you don't come, I'll burn down this village."

The boy looked around at the terrified faces of the villagers. Then his eyes met Katara's. "I'll go with you," he said softly. "Don't hurt anyone."

Two Fire Nation soldiers grabbed the boy and roughly herded him toward their ship. Sokka and Katara both ran after him.

A firebender lifted his leg and kicked out swiftly. The movement sent a column of flames from a nearby cooking fire rushing toward them. "Stay back!" the firebender shouted as the fire passed just inches above their heads. They stopped and watched helplessly as the soldiers dragged the boy away.

Prince Zuko and his troops marched back onto their ship. Its mighty engines roared to life, and the fleet departed as quickly as they had arrived.

As Sokka and Katara headed back to their igloo, a mournful wailing sound filled the air.

Inside their igloo, Sokka paced back and forth, fingering his boomerang and trying to figure out what, if anything, to do next.

"That Prince Zuko," Katara snarled. "If I ever see him again, he and I are going to have a real problem."

Outside, Appa once again wailed in distress.

"They were looking for someone old," Sokka said, continuing his nervous pacing. "Then, for some reason, they realized it was this boy they wanted."

Again, Appa's mournful cry drifted into the igloo.

Katara sat, fuming. "That prince walked around like he owned our village," she said angrily. "When are we going to stand up to them? We can't just let them take whoever they want. They took Mom the same way." She paused as memories of her mother flooded her mind. This time she chose to focus on the ones that fueled her rage. "We have to save that boy, Sokka," she said, the conviction clear in her voice.

Sokka stopped his pacing and thought hard. "How are we supposed to get to him?" he asked. "They're on a ship. They're miles away by now. We can paddle all we want in our canoe, but we're never going to catch them."

Appa's cries sounded again, but this time they were accompanied by the sounds of children laughing and shrieking with joy. Sokka and Katara looked at each other for a moment, wondering what was going on. They stepped out of their igloo to see.

The sight that greeted them outside caused them both to stare in stunned amazement. Appa was floating several feet off the ground. Village children hung from his legs and tail, screeching with delight.

"His bison-creature-thing floats," Katara said, her eyes wide open with delight.

Sokka smiled. "Now *that* could probably catch the ship," he said, a plan already forming in his mind.

"All we have to do is convince Grandma to let us go," Katara said. "Come on."

They rushed back to their igloo and began gathering supplies. In addition to clothing, cooking items, and sleeping rolls, Katara also took a small leather pouch filled with water. Sokka brought his boomerang.

They stopped next at their grandmother's igloo, where they found her stirring a bubbling stew in a large iron pot.

"Are you going to try to stop us, Grandma?" Katara asked when she had finished explaining their plan.

"Sit down, children," Grandma said.

Sokka and Katara glanced at each other, then sat down on either side of her.

"Do you believe we all have a destiny?" Grandma asked.

Sokka and Katara both nodded.

"I knew from the moment we discovered you were a bender, Katara, that I would one day learn your destiny," Grandma continued. "There hasn't been a waterbender in the Southern Water Tribe since my friend Hamma was taken away. Today, I realized your destiny."

Katara felt her stomach tense up, yet her mind raced with possibilities.

"Did you see that boy's tattoos?" Grandma asked.

"Tattoos like that haven't been seen in almost a century. I could be wrong, but I believe they are airbending tattoos." She paused for a moment, stirring the pot of stew and allowing the significance of what she had just said to sink in. Then she continued. "Sokka and Katara, I think you may have found the Avatar."

Her grandchildren remained still, unable to speak, their minds reeling from this announcement.

She continued. "The fact that you found him tells me that your destinies are tied to his. He will need you two. And we all need him."

She stopped stirring and leaned in close to her grandchildren. "Now I could be wrong," she said, smiling for the first time. "But I think you're about to go on a great adventure. Promise me one thing, though—that you will both come back to me safely."

Sokka and Katara leaned into their grandmother's arms. Katara thought about the daunting task ahead, but also about how much she loved her brother and her grandmother. The three of them held one another tightly in a warm embrace that none of them wanted to end.

CHAPTER 3

The tattooed boy sat on the floor of the prison room aboard Prince Zuko's Fire Nation warship. He wasn't sure how he would get out of this room or off this ship, but he did know that he had done the right thing by giving himself up to save an entire village full of people.

The monks had taught him well, and their values and rules were now an integral part of who he was. There were lives at stake, and now they were safe. That was all that mattered. He took a deep breath and continued to meditate.

Suddenly the door to the prison room swung open. In walked Prince Zuko, accompanied by a man in his early fifties. The man's gray hair was so long, it reached the middle of his back, and his eyes radiated a gentle kindness.

The prince remained in the corner of the room, hidden among the shadows. The older man approached the boy.

"What do you want with me?" the boy asked softly.

"My nephew wants me to perform a little test on you," the man said. His voice sounded as kind as his face appeared.

"What kind of test?" the boy asked suspiciously.

"I assure you it won't hurt," the man said. "I've performed it hundreds of times. It will only take a few minutes, then you will be free to go."

The boy stared hard at the older man, then glanced toward the prince, who remained in the shadows. Zuko said nothing.

"Would you mind if I put a few things in front of you?" the man continued, gesturing to a small table in the center of the room. "It will only take a moment."

"That's all you want?" the boy asked, trying to figure out exactly what was going on.

"That is all," the man said. "My name is Iroh, and you have my word."

The boy nodded, still unsure of what was to come. He stood, then walked to the table and took a seat.

Iroh went to the corner of the room and brought back a tray on which sat three objects. He placed the tray on the table in front of the boy. He took the first item, a candle, and lit it. The flame flickered and danced atop the wax pillar. The man then placed the candle directly in front of the boy. The flame stopped flickering at once. It grew long and thin and perfectly still. Iroh moved his hand slightly, and the flame went out.

Next he picked up a small jug of water and poured a small amount out onto the table. It spread in all directions, creating an irregularly shaped puddle. Then, after a moment, the water began to move, forming into a perfect circle. Iroh stared at the boy, then turned to look at his nephew in the corner. He wiped the water off the table.

Iroh took the final object, a small slender rock, from the tray. He balanced the rock on its thin edge and let go. The rock stayed perfectly balanced on its edge when all logic and the laws of gravity said it should have toppled over.

Prince Zuko stepped from the shadows, walking right up to the boy and breaking the long silence in the room.

"You are my prisoner, boy," he snarled. "I'm taking you back to the Fire Nation."

The confused boy looked directly at Iroh. "But you said I could—"

"I apologize," Iroh said, clearly upset at having to break his word. "I should have explained that if you failed the test, as all others did, you would have been free to leave. But as it turns out, you are the only one in the entire world who could pass." He paused for a moment, then brought his hands together in front of him and bowed slightly. "It is truly an honor to be in your presence."

Prince Zuko shoved past his uncle. "Don't even try to escape," he warned the boy. "This is a warship. The room is made entirely of impregnable metal. There are armed guards outside the room, and my uncle and I are expert firebenders. So any thought you have of escape is—"

The boy moved with astonishing swiftness. He leaped to his feet, kicked off from his chair with one foot, then sprung off the table with his other, floating as if weightless. He landed with his back to the door, which opened inward into the room.

"Stop!" cried Zuko. "There is no way you can—"

The boy brought his hands together in a smooth, practiced motion and pushed them forward. Immediately a powerful gust of wind rushed through the room. The force of the wind tossed the boy backward through the open doorway, then slammed the door shut on Zuko and Iroh.

Out in the hallway a group of Fire Nation guards pointed their spears at the boy. He planted his feet and began pulling at the air in a hand-over-hand motion, as if he were pulling an invisible rope. Violently rushing air tore through the hallway, pinning the guards against the wall. The boy rode the speeding wind currents down the hall, snatching his staff as he passed it.

Bounding up a set of metal stairs, he emerged out onto the deck of the mighty warship. The ship slid slowly through a narrow ice valley, making its way toward the vast ocean.

The metallic clang of footsteps rang out behind him. The

boy looked around. He was trapped. He had nowhere to go.

From above came a familiar and welcoming sound—the unmistakable sound of a sky bison.

"Urrraaarrr," wailed Appa.

"Appa!" cried the boy. Looking up he spotted Appa standing on a high ridge of ice ahead of the ship. Seated on the bison's back were Sokka and Katara.

Fire Nation guards burst from the stairwell, followed closely by Zuko and Iroh. The boy flicked his wrists, shaking his staff. Two wings emerged from either side of the long pole.

"Don't move!" ordered Zuko. "You have nowhere to run."

The boy dashed toward the edge of the ship, picking up speed with every step. Although he reached the edge, he kept going, running right off the deck. He disappeared from view, but the expected splash of him crashing into the ocean never came.

"What?" the prince cried out. "Where? He's gone. Where did he go?"

The boy suddenly reappeared, rising up into the sky, gliding along on his winged staff, like a bird riding the air currents.

From the deck of his ship, Prince Zuko watched the boy fly toward the sky bison, who was waiting on the nearby ledge.

"I underestimated him, Uncle, because he looked like a boy," the prince said bitterly. "I won't do that again." He shook his head, furious at himself. "I had him, Uncle. For a moment I had my honor back."

Iroh placed a hand gently onto his nephew's shoulder. "It's not by chance that for generations, people have been searching for him, and that you were the one to see that light and find him," he said softly, trying to comfort the distraught prince. "Your destinies are tied, Zuko. That I can be sure of. But where has the Avatar been for a hundred years?"

CHAPTER 4

The young airbender drifted down through the sky, using the air currents for resistance, until he landed on Appa's back.

"Urrraaarrr," the sky bison wailed happily.

"It's good to see you too, buddy," the boy answered gleefully, scratching the huge beast on the top of his furry head. Then he turned to Sokka and Katara, who sat behind him. The two just stared at him in shock.

"You came just in time," the boy said. "Thanks."

"Oh, I'm Katara. That's my brother, Sokka," Katara told the boy.

"Grandma was right," Sokka said in amazement. "You can bend air. How do you do that?"

"We airbenders learn to feel the energy behind the wind, not just the breeze on our skin," the boy explained.

"It's all about controlling energy."

The young airbender looked down at Prince Zuko's ship, which moved swiftly through the ice valley below.

"The Fire Nation is up to something," he said, frowning. "I have to go back home now. I could drop you guys back at your village, or you can come with me and I'll bring you back home later."

Sokka and Katara looked at each other. They both thought of their grandmother's words. Their destinies were now tied to the young airbender's. They had committed to helping him, and they were going to see that promise through.

"We're going to make sure you get back safely," Katara said.

"Yeah, drop us back home later," Sokka added quickly.

"Great," said the boy, obviously pleased to have his new friends along on the journey. "Then let's go home, Appa. Yip-yip!"

Appa moaned his approval, then stepped off the ice cliff, lifting his enormous bulk into the air. The three passengers seated on his back held on tightly as the sky bison flew out over the ocean. Within a few moments, the Fire Nation ship had disappeared from view.

"This is so much fun!" Sokka cried as they soared through the sky. "In a terrifying kind of a way."

"'Yip-yip'?" Katara asked.

"That's the command to start flying," the airbender replied, looking out ahead as warm thoughts of home filled his mind.

A few hours later the Southern Air Temple came into view.

"There it is!" the boy cried excitedly, pointing at a grand temple that sat high atop a mountain. "Home. Bring us down, Appa, old buddy."

Appa landed in a big open field near the base of the Southern Air Temple. Katara and Sokka dropped from the bison's back, landing hard on the ground. The young airbender drifted softly down beside them.

"Katara, this field is where the flying sky bison sleep," he explained. Looking around, he saw no sky bison. "That's weird. They must all be out flying, I guess."

Katara glanced all around. "Wow," she said. "I didn't know people lived so high up in the mountains."

Leaving Appa, the trio hiked up the winding mountain path toward the temple. Its many towers rose majestically, each of which were topped by a gleaming spire jutting into the sky. The boy practically ran every step of the way. Sokka and Katara did their best to keep up, but they lagged behind, winded by the steep climb.

Reaching the temple's courtyard, the boy dashed across the open plaza and leaped onto a raised stone platform.

"Hey, Chinto! Monae! I'm back!" he shouted. The only answer he got was his own voice echoing among the towers. "Guys? Hey, guys, I want you to meet some new friends of mine!"

Again his shouts were met with nothing but echoes. Confused, he raced from one end of the courtyard to the other, searching. A few moments later his two companions joined him in the courtyard.

"Hey, baldy, stop running so fast," Sokka said, trying to catch his breath.

Katara looked around at the magnificent temple. "This is where you live?" she asked in amazement.

The young airbender nodded. "They must be playing a trick on me or something," he said anxiously. "Monk Gyatso is probably going to jump out at any second, to try and scare me. He's the teacher responsible for me. He's kind of like my father."

Katara was about to ask him a question, but realized that after all this time she had never asked the boy his name. "Is it okay if you tell me your name?" she asked curiously.

"The monks named me Aang," the young airbender replied, glancing at Katara. Then he started searching the courtyard again. "Okay, guys, enough. A joke's a joke, but this has gone too far."

Suddenly, something scurried out from behind a wall.

"It's a spider-rat!" Sokka shrieked, snatching his boomerang from his pack.

"They're poisonous. Everyone get behind me. I'll deal with this."

"No, no, Sokka," Aang cried. "He's a flying lemur-bat. We keep them as pets."

The small white creature stopped and stared at Aang.

He had long, pointed ears; two giant wings; a dark face with piercing amber eyes; and a striped tail.

Sokka put away his boomerang and leaned in close to Katara. "I didn't think there were any lemur-bats left," he whispered.

"Weren't lemur-bats extinct a long time ago, Aang?" she asked.

"Extinct?" Aang replied in shock. "What do you mean? There must be thousands of them on this mountain."

It was then that Katara realized just how long Aang had been trapped inside that ice. She also realized that he had absolutely no idea how long he had been gone.

"Aang, your friends were airbending monks?" she asked nervously.

Aang's face suddenly brightened. "What time is it?" he asked, glancing up at the gathering dusk. "I know where they all are right now. They're in the prayer field." He bounded back down the stairs, five at a time.

"Aang, wait!" Katara cried, chasing after him. "I have to talk to you."

When Katara reached the bottom of the stairs, she found Aang staring in disbelief at a large field. He stood there motionless, shocked by what came into view.

The field was littered with bones, helmets, armor, weapons, and war machines. Katara recognized the uniforms and equipment as those of the Fire Nation. Aang knew the garments that clothed the skeletons were those of the monks who had raised him. The young airbender clutched his head and shook it in despair.

"Aang, I have to tell you something," Katara said softly. "I think you were in that ice for almost a hundred years. And after you disappeared, the Fire Nation started a war."

Aang continued to stare out at the prayer field, refusing to make eye contact with her.

"But I only left here a few days ago," he finally said, his voice quaking.

"Aang, the Fire Nation knew that the Avatar would be born into the Air Nomads," Katara explained. "So they—they exterminated all the Air Nomads."

Aang stumbled forward, tripped over a pile of bones, then regained his balance. He turned to face Katara, anger flashing in his eyes. "You're lying!" he shouted, choked with rage.

He ran out into the field and froze at the sight of a skeleton dressed in monk's robes. Around its bony neck rested a round medallion, crudely carved from wood, held in place by a necklace of beads.

"This is Monk Gyatso's," Aang said, barely able to get the words out. "I—I made it for him."

Katara walked up behind Aang and placed a hand on his shoulder, hoping to comfort him.

"No!" he shouted, turning swiftly to face her.

Katara stumbled back, shocked by the fury in Aang's face. She backed away and watched in confusion as Aang's eyes and then his tattoos started to glow.

"Aang?" she said cautiously. "Are you all right?"

A funnel of wind began swirling violently all around Aang, blowing bones and charred battle gear into the air. The spinning vortex pushed Katara away, but she fought against its force, trying to stay close to Aang.

Arriving at the prayer field, Sokka was stunned by the sight of the small gentle boy glowing, surrounded by a tiny tornado.

"Katara, stay away from him!" he cried, battling the wind with each step. Sokka reached Katara, took her by the arm, and pulled her away from Aang. The two watched in terror and amazement as Aang floated up into the air, hovering in the middle of the funnel of wind.

Inside the swirling vortex, Aang felt the world start to blur. He felt confused, although not frightened, and he was not sure where he was. The landscape was still and silent, covered with a thick white mist.

A scraping sound startled him. Aang walked slowly toward the sound, stepping blindly through the fog.

He came face-to-face with an enormous beast with scaly skin. The creature was rubbing up against the rough wall, creating the scraping sound. Suddenly it stopped moving.

"Avatar," the Dragon said in a deep but gentle voice. "The human world and the spirit world are in danger. Where have you been? You may already be too late."

Then the Dragon disappeared as quickly as he had

come, but Aang remained shrouded in the white mist. Somewhere, far away in the distance, a girl's voice rang out.

"I know you feel alone, Aang. I know how you feel. My mother was taken and killed by the Fire Nation. I know you feel you don't have a family anymore. But Sokka and I can be your family, Aang. I'm your friend. I'm here. I won't leave you!"

The white mist started to slowly lift. The prayer field came back into Aang's view, along with Sokka and Katara, as he hovered in the air. He felt himself drift toward the ground as the winds all around him died down. He landed and felt as if he was going to pass out.

Then he collapsed into Katara's waiting arms.

"I'm sorry, Aang," she said. "I'm so sorry."

CHAPTER 5

A massive Fire Nation warship cut through the churning, whitecapped ocean. Out on the deck, a guard looked through a telescope at a second ship just a short distance away. A tall, muscular man stepped onto the deck. His penetrating brown eyes peered out from a strong, fierce-looking face.

The guard immediately stood at attention. "Commander Zhao, we've found him, sir," the guard said crisply.

The commander peered into the telescope and spotted a smaller Fire Nation ship. On its deck stood Prince Zuko.

"The banished prince," Commander Zhao said, smirking. "Let's offer him lunch."

Zhao ordered his crew to maneuver their vessel closer to Zuko's ship.

"Prince Zuko!" Commander Zhao shouted from the deck when they had pulled alongside the smaller ship. "Why don't you and your uncle join us here for lunch? We would be honored to have you as our guests."

A short while later Commander Zhao and his guards gathered in the ship's main mess hall. The guards laughed loudly and swapped stories between bites of food. Seated at the commander's table, Zuko and Iroh looked cautiously at the group as they ate their meal.

Commander Zhao stood, and the room went silent.

"I wanted to thank the great General Iroh and the young Prince Zuko for dining with us," he began. "I remember watching Prince Zuko playing with all the little girls when he was a boy."

Zuko clenched his jaw and balled his hand into a fist.

Zhao continued. "As you all know, the Fire Lord banished his son and will not let him return to the throne—unless he finds the Avatar."

Commander Zhao bent over and looked under the table. "Wait, Prince Zuko," he said in a mocking tone. "I think I see the Avatar. He's been hiding under this table for one hundred years. No wonder you couldn't find him."

The guards in the mess hall looked at one another and stifled their laughter.

"I have found him!" Zuko announced emphatically.

The guards exploded with laughter as all eyes turned to the prince.

"The Avatar was killed in the raid on the Air Nomads and was never reborn," Zhao said, his tone turning deadly serious. "Don't tell such lies."

Zuko's hands began to tremble. The flames on all the candles on Zuko's table started bending toward him, growing larger as his anger increased. Seeing this, Iroh put a comforting hand on his nephew's arm. Zuko took a deep breath, and the candles settled.

But Commander Zhao was not finished. "You may wonder why the wise and honorable Fire Lord would send his son on this impossible task when the entire Fire Nation has been searching for the Avatar for a hundred years and has found nothing. Well, sometimes children need to be taught a lesson, because they don't know how to behave. I commend the Fire Lord's discipline. For example, it seems that I need to remind Prince Zuko that during his banishment, he is considered an enemy of the Fire Nation and is not allowed to wear the uniform of a Fire Nation soldier."

Zhao stared straight at Zuko, who squirmed uncomfortably in his seat.

"But we will let him wear it today," Zhao continued. "Like a child in a costume."

Zuko could take no more. He shoved his chair away from the table and stood defiantly, looking Commander Zhao right in the eyes. "One day my father will take me back," he hissed. "And you will bow down before me."

Then he turned and rushed from the mess hall.

Iroh stood and bowed at his host. "Thank you for the delicious food and hospitality, Commander," he said. Then he followed his nephew down a ladder and back onto his own ship.

"We have to hunt him down, Uncle," Zuko said, staring back up at the larger warship. "Before anyone else finds him first."

The great sky bison flew through the air, heading from the Southern Air Temple to a forest on the edge of the Earth Kingdom, with Katara, Sokka, and Aang on his back. There they set up camp. Aang sat off by himself, still trying to make sense of what he had just seen at the temple and of his bizarre journey to the spirit world.

Katara worried about him. She saw how devastated he was about coming to terms with the loss of everyone he had ever known and loved. And then there was the display of glowing and wind in the prayer field. Was that what all airbenders did? How could she know? Aang was the last of his kind.

"Are you okay?" she asked Aang, walking over and sitting beside him. Sokka got up and joined his sister at Aang's side.

Aang just nodded.

"You know," she said, "my grandmother thinks because you're an airbender that you might be the Avatar."

Aang ignored her comment. "How much does the Fire Nation control?" he asked.

"A lot of villages in the Earth Kingdom, like around here," she explained. "They haven't been able to conquer the big cities, like Ba Sing Se, but they are making plans, I'm sure."

Sokka, never as patient as his sister, couldn't stand it anymore. "So, are you the Avatar, Aang?" he asked bluntly.

Aang nodded his head, but remained silent. Sokka and Katara also sat quietly, trying to absorb this incredible news.

"Whoa," Sokka said, finally breaking the silence.

"Unbelievable," Katara added.

"But I have to tell you guys something," Aang said urgently.

Before Aang could continue, a young boy burst out of the woods, his face filled with terror. Spotting the trio, the boy stopped and glanced back over his shoulder.

"What is this?" Sokka asked suspiciously, scrambling to his feet along with the others.

A group of Fire Nation soldiers stepped from the woods at the same spot where the boy had come out. Sokka grabbed his boomerang. Katara struck a waterbending stance and fingered the small water pouch that hung from her waist.

"Stay hidden," Katara whispered to Aang, who immediately pulled the hood of his cloak up over his head and turned to face away from the soldiers.

The leader of the soldiers pointed at the frightened boy. "That child is being arrested," the soldier announced.

"For what?" Katara asked.

"He was bending tiny stones at us from behind a tree," the soldier explained, rubbing his head. "It really hurt, too."

"He can bend earth?" Katara asked curiously.

"Earthbending is forbidden in this village," the soldier blustered. "By order of the Fire Lord."

"Leave him alone," Katara said through tightly clenched teeth. "You're not taking him anywhere."

Sokka immediately grabbed the boy by the shoulders and pulled him behind his back. "No one's taking anyone away," he announced defiantly. The boy peeked out from behind Sokka.

Katara stepped forward and opened her water pouch. In one smooth motion she raised her hands and spread her fingers wide. Water rose up out of the water pouch and spread into the shape of a fan. Then it froze into solid ice, shifted back to liquid, and froze again.

"She's a bender!" one of the soldiers cried.

Katara pulled her hands back, then whipped them forward toward the soldiers, hoping to use her frozen fan to attack. "Yiiiiii!" she yelled as she unleashed her waterbending move. But the water didn't fly forward as she had hoped. Turning around to see what happened, she saw Sokka's arms and chest wrapped in ice.

"Katara," he whined, trying in vain to break free.

The soldiers moved quickly, slapping handcuffs on Sokka, Katara, Aang, and the young earthbending boy. The flying lemur-bat Aang had befriended at the Southern Air Temple and named Momo was sitting on his shoulder. Katara unfroze the water that covered Sokka and returned it to her water pouch.

"You need to get better at bending water before you pull something like that," Sokka grumbled angrily as the soldiers led them through a small Earth Kingdom village.

"Okay, leave me alone, Sokka," Katara replied, feeling terrible about what she'd done. "I'm sorry."

Peering out from under the hood of his cloak, Aang looked around at the village. The houses were falling apart. The roads were broken and uneven. Poor children in ragged clothes lined the street. He was shocked by the conditions. It was all wrong! The people of the Earth Kingdom were proud and self-sufficient. They wouldn't have let this happen. This was obviously the result of poor treatment by the occupying Fire Nation army.

The soldiers led the group to a prison camp they had set up just outside the village. The three friends and the Earth Kingdom boy were shoved through a gateway of a tall metal fence. The gate slammed shut behind them.

Inside the prison yard, Aang saw men from the Earth Kingdom village sitting on the ground, huddled in blankets. They looked weary and defeated. The boy who had been captured with them ran to his father, who sat in a corner.

The man hugged the child close to him.

"This is my dad," the boy said.

"Hello," the father greeted them sadly.

"The Fire Nation's plan is obviously to suppress all other bending," Sokka whispered to Aang.

"How did this happen to your village?" Aang asked the man.

"The Fire Nation sent soldiers," the man explained. "We fought them and defeated them. But then they sent their machines. Huge machines made of metal. There was nothing we could do. Even earthbenders can't bend metal. Those who could not bend were allowed to live in peace if we benders were imprisoned."

Aang was shocked. He refused to accept that these powerful people were helpless. He decided to inspire them to action. Stepping to the center of the prison yard, still careful to keep his tattoos hidden, Aang addressed the prisoners.

"Earthbenders!" he shouted. "You don't know me, but I know you. My teacher used to tell me stories about your courage."

All eyes in the prison yard turned toward the strange, hooded boy. A few of the Fire Nation guards positioned outside the fence turned to see what was happening as well.

"Why are you acting this way?" Aang continued, his tone growing defiant. "You are powerful, amazing people.

You don't need to live like this. There is earth right beneath your feet. The ground is an extension of who you are."

Some prisoners grumbled. Others waved their hands dismissively. Most turned away. They had been disheartened for so long.

The Fire Nation guards who had been listening looked at one another and laughed. Katara's eyes filled with tears at the hopelessness of these people and at Aang's efforts to rouse them to action.

Realizing that he was losing his audience, Aang shouted, "If the Avatar had returned, would that mean anything to you?"

The Fire Nation guards immediately stopped laughing. A few of the prisoners turned back toward Aang.

"The Avatar is dead!" one of them yelled back.

"If he was here, he would protect us!" shouted another.

Aang locked eyes with Katara as if he was silently letting her know what was coming next. Then he turned back to the prisoners.

"My name is Aang," he cried. "And I am the Avatar!"

The prison yard fell silent.

"I ran away," Aang continued. "I'm sorry. But I'm back now."

An urgent murmuring spread through the yard. The Fire Nation guards rushed through the gate and surrounded Aang. He looked around from guard to guard, maintaining a serious expression.

"It's time for you to stop doing this," he told them firmly.

"The Avatar would have to be an airbender," one of the guards said, sneering at Aang. "Are you an airbender, boy?"

The guards all laughed loudly and derisively.

"I think not, boy," the guard cackled. "We killed all the airbenders, so the Avatar will never return."

"Not *all* the airbenders," Aang announced. He threw off his cloak, revealing his tattoos. The guards immediately took a step back, stunned. The earthbending prisoners let out a collective gasp at the sight of the small bald boy and his airbending tattoos.

"I am the Last Airbender," Aang said proudly.

The guards charged Aang at once, but the boy was too quick. He jumped into the air, spinning like a top, and floated up, creating a whirlwind below him that flung the guards back in all directions. Seeing this, the earthbenders stood, their eyes opened wide.

"It's true," one of the prisoners cried. "The Avatar has returned. He has come to save us!"

Gaining confidence once again, the earthbenders unleashed their powers, bending earth against the Fire Nation guards to help the Avatar.

Aang stood ready for the next attack. The guards slowly climbed to their feet, stared at him for a moment, then turned and ran from the prison yard.

A huge cheer rose up from the prisoners as they watched the Fire Nation guards flee the prison. Sokka joined the celebrating earthbenders.

"Way to go, Aang," he cried.

"Thank you, Avatar," said the father of the earthbending boy. "You have given us back our hope." Then he joined his fellow earthbenders as they left the prison yard and headed back to their village.

Katara embraced Aang. "You know, Aang, he's right," she said when the two joined Sokka. "The greatest thing you have to offer is hope."

Aang pondered that thought as he and his friends left the prison, heading back to the forest where Appa was waiting for them.

CHAPTER 6

Traveling deeper into the Earth Kingdom, Aang, Sokka, and Katara left Appa just outside a small village and strolled into the center of the tiny town. Aang had thought about Katara's words and decided that she was right. At the moment, hope was what he had to offer to the defeated and oppressed people of the world. He had made up his mind. He was going to let everyone know that the Avatar had returned.

As he entered the village, Aang threw back his hood, revealing his tattoos. Townspeople stared at him and pointed. Aang waved and smiled. "Hello," he said. "Hi. Hello."

The group paused at a courtyard in the oldest section of the town that was in front of a tall weather-beaten statue of a beautiful woman wearing a kimono and holding a fan.

A faded plaque at the base of the statue read: AVATAR KYOSHI.

An old man, his shoulders stooped with age, his long hair thin and white, stepped from the crowd that had gathered. He looked right at Aang and bowed respectfully.

"This was you when you were born an earthbender two lifetimes ago," the old man said. "You came to our village. You played with the children. Avatar Kyoshi loved games."

"I do too," Aang said quickly. "I mean, I still do." The idea of living many lives and being reborn was going to take some getting used to.

"When they invaded our village, the Fire Nation forbade us from having anything related to bending," the old man explained. "Now you have inspired us."

Aang watched as the people of the village brought out their traditional earthbending robes and belts, then slipped them on over their tattered clothing. The finely made and beautifully decorated garments seemed to fill them with a newfound spirit.

Then, one by one, earthbenders unleashed powerful moves. One bender raised his hands over his head and a tall peak of rock sprung up from the earth. Another earthbender whipped her arms forward and an enormous boulder flew through the air, coming to rest on top of the peak the first earthbender had raised.

Aang was thrilled that just his presence had filled these people with hope and renewed their fighting spirit. Then a terrifying thought popped into his mind.

Aang turned and ran from the crowd and quickly caught up with Katara and Sokka on a quiet street on the outskirts of the village.

"What is it, Aang?" Katara asked.

Aang looked to the sky. "I ran away before they trained me to be the Avatar," he confessed. "I don't know how to bend the other elements."

Sokka and Katara looked at each other, stunned by this news.

"Why did you run away, Aang?" Katara asked softly.

"The day they told me I was the Avatar, they also told me that I couldn't have a family," Aang explained. "They warned me never to fall in love. They said it can't work with the responsibilities of the Avatar."

Katara stared at Aang sadly. "Why can't the Avatar have a family?"

"I asked that," Aang replied. "They said that's the sacrifice the Avatar always has to make."

"Okay, so what if we find you teachers to teach you bending?" Sokka asked. His voice was upbeat, hoping to break the gloomy mood that had descended on Aang and his sister. "Which element would you have to learn first?

"Water," Aang replied. "The cycle is Air, Water, Earth, Fire."

"Hmm," Sokka said thoughtfully, resting his hand under his chin—his favorite thinking position. "We don't have any waterbenders in the Southern Water Tribe. Except Katara, of course, but she couldn't teach anybody."

"Hey!" Katara shouted, scowling at her brother.

"I'm just saying," Sokka whined. "You're like a baby bender."

"Hey!" Katara repeated.

"But there are really powerful benders in the Northern Water Tribe," Sokka said. "My dad told me about it before he left. They are led by a princess. There will be teachers there for sure, but they're all the way on the other side of the world."

"We can get there on Appa," Aang suggested, his spirits starting to lift.

"That's what I was thinking," Sokka said. "And maybe we could stop in the villages along the way. Start a change in the war in these small villages, like you did in that prison and just now in the Kyoshi village. That's how you win a war. Not just by fighting on the big fronts, but also by building support from the inside."

Sokka glanced at Katara and spotted a big grin on her face. "What?" he asked, shrugging.

"I didn't know you were so smart," Katara quipped.

"Thanks," he said. Then he paused and thought for a moment and added, "I think."

And so the group set out on their journey to find Aang a waterbending teacher in the Northern Water Tribe. They flew across the Earth Kingdom on Appa, heading north. Along the way they landed in villages across the Earth

Kingdom, where Aang announced that he was back.

He got the same reaction everywhere he went. For the first time in years the villagers grew hopeful that the Fire Nation might actually be defeated. In villages where they encountered Fire Nation soldiers, Aang used his airbending to defeat them and free the village from their grip.

In one small town near the northern border of the Earth Kingdom, a group of villagers locked arms to form a circle around Aang. Sokka and Katara joined the group and happily danced around their friend.

"Welcome back, Avatar," one villager said.

"With your help we can defeat the Fire Nation!" shouted another.

Aang took in the joyful spirit of the people as they danced around him. The confidence he had once again inspired in a tiny town brought him hope that he really could do what everyone believed he could.

When it was time to move on, they made their way to the edge of the village where Appa was waiting. A crowd of villagers waved and shouted as the three friends climbed up onto the great sky bison.

Three mysterious figures, draped in green cloaks and holding metal fans, stepped forward from the crowd and stared at Sokka, Katara, and Aang. Then they fanned themselves casually and dropped back into the crowd.

"What was that about?" Sokka asked. "Does anyone else get the feeling that we're being watched?"

Aang ignored the question. He had more pressing things to worry about. "Yip-yip!" he cried as Appa took off into the sky. "We've got to get to the Northern Water Tribe as fast as we can," Aang said urgently.

CHAPTER 7

Commander Zhao walked slowly along a path leading through a field of golden grass. Before him he could see the sun setting behind the Fire Lord's magnificent palace, its stone and tile spires rising high into the crimson-tinged sky.

Zhao approached a man who was sitting on a bench, looking out at the palace and its vast grounds. Stopping a few feet away, Zhao paused, lowered his head respectfully, and waited for the other man to speak first.

"Are the stories real or not, Commander?" the seated man asked.

"Fire Lord Ozai, we are tracking the stories of the Avatar through the towns," Zhao replied. "There have been many sightings of him. Some say he is just a skinny boy."

The Fire Lord looked up at Zhao, who continued to

speak. "But, my lord, there seems to be a growing rebellion inspired by this boy. How seriously should we take this? He is just one person. The reign of the Avatar is over."

Fire Lord Ozai looked back toward his palace. "The Avatar will convince others that the four elements are the same," he said. "He will confine us to a lower place, where Fire will no longer be the dominant element. Others will feel more powerful. And he will once again be the bridge to the spirit world."

"Then this is a Fire Nation issue now," Zhao stated with certainty. "It can no longer simply be about punishing your son, who has demonstrated questionable courage." The Fire Lord said nothing, so Zhao continued. "I believe we should set a trap for the Avatar. He will return to the Northern Air Temple to try to contact the spirit world. I am certain of it. I will send word ahead to have our men wait there. I will start my travel now, if you give me permission."

Again the Fire Lord said nothing, and Zhao grew uncomfortable by the extended silence. "Forgive my boldness, my lord, but I found the Great Library when most said it didn't even exist," Zhao said. "Because of my actions, we have now learned all the secrets of the spirit world contained within the library. With all due respect, I believe I have earned this command. I have earned the right to find and eliminate the Avatar."

The Fire Lord nodded and finally spoke. "My son deserves the opportunity to regain his honor. But you may also pursue the Avatar with your army. If you should find him first, then that is simply my son's fate."

Commander Zhao bowed deeply. "As always, my lord, I think you are being extremely fair," he said. "I will leave at once." Then he turned and strode from the palace, a satisfied smirk spreading across his broad face.

Prince Zuko and his uncle Iroh sat in a tea shop in the Earth Kingdom. Even though the colony was set up by the Fire Nation, Zuko made sure his face was hidden by the hood of his cloak. It was his usual state these days.

"We're close, Uncle," the prince said softly. "The Avatar and his friends are moving north. We're catching up to them."

Iroh took a sip from his steaming cup of jasmine tea and looked at his nephew. "There are a lot of pretty girls in this town, Zuko," he said, placing his cup onto the table. "You could fall in love here. We could both settle down here and have a good life." Then lowering his voice he added, "We don't have to continue this."

Zuko's face, so full of hope a moment ago, hardened. "We must continue, Uncle," he said. "I'll show you why."

He called out to a little boy who was walking past them. "Hey, little one, come here." The boy stepped up to their table.

"You look like a smart boy," Zuko said, keeping his face well hidden. "Tell me what you know about the prince, the Fire Lord's son."

"He did something wrong," the boy replied.

"He spoke out of turn to a general in defense of some of his friends who were going to be sacrificed in a battle," Zuko explained.

"Then Prince Zuko was sentenced to an Agni-Ki duel," the boy continued the story. "But when he showed up, it was his father he was to fight. But he would not fight his father."

"His father mocked him," Zuko continued, a touch of emotion creeping into his voice. "His father said, 'I should bring your sister up here to beat you.'"

"Then the father burned his son to teach him a lesson," the boy said casually, as if he were repeating a history lesson he had learned in school.

Trying hard to rein in his rising anger, Zuko then asked, "What would you feel if you were Prince Zuko?"

"Ashamed."

"Why?"

The boy paused and thought about the question for a moment. "Because I would have no honor," he replied.

Zuko nodded, and the boy hurried off to join his mother.

Zuko's hands were shaking with rage as he reached for his teacup. "*That* is why we must catch the Avatar first, Uncle," he whispered. "And then we can think about pretty girls."

Aang and Katara stood at the shore of a sparkling lake beside a forest. Nearby, Sokka tended to a campfire.

The group had landed for the night, on their way to the Northern Water Tribe. At the edge of the forest, Appa rested from many long days of flying. He curled up into a fuzzy white ball and snored loudly.

At the water's edge, Katara pulled a scroll from her bag and unrolled it. On the scroll were drawings of a figure performing waterbending forms. "This was a gift from a group of earthbenders. They gave it to me as we were leaving their village," she explained as she and Aang looked over the drawings. "It might help you as you start to practice your waterbending. Let's try it together."

Aang and Katara moved their arms from side to side in a gentle sweeping motion. "Try to keep your wrists bent, like in the drawing," Katara said. "Let's try it again."

They repeated the movement, but again Aang failed to correctly bend his wrists. "What's wrong, Aang?" Katara asked. "You seem really distracted today, like your mind really isn't on waterbending."

Aang glanced across the lake to the north. "I saw those maps Sokka picked up. We're near the Northern Air Temple," he said. Then he turned to look at her. "Do you think it would be okay if I just visited there and came back? I'd be back in less than a day."

"Why do you want to go there?" Katara asked.

"I had a vision at the Southern Air Temple," Aang explained. "I talked to a dragon spirit who I think can help us. I believe that if I go to another spiritual place, I can get back to the spirit world and talk to the Dragon Spirit again."

"I don't know, Aang," Katara said warily. "Let's see what Sokka thinks."

A short while later Katara filled Sokka in on what Aang wanted to do.

"I'm not sure that's a great idea," Sokka told his sister. "We started a rebellion. The Northern Water Tribe is in jeopardy. I think we should try to get there as fast as we can, without delay. Try to talk him out of it, okay?"

Katara vowed to talk to Aang later.

That night, as Sokka and Katara slept, Aang slipped quietly over to Appa and awakened the slumbering bison, who shook himself and slowly rose to his feet. Then, climbing up onto Appa's back, Aang grabbed the reins. "Yip-yip," he whispered, and Appa once again took to the sky.

The sound of rushing air created by Appa's liftoff woke up Sokka and Katara.

"I guess your little talk didn't convince him," Sokka said.

"He should be back in less than day," Katara explained.

"You realize the Fire Nation's been following us?" Sokka said with concern. "If we make a wrong move, they'll catch us. And more importantly, they'll catch him."

Then the brother and sister watched as Appa and Aang disappeared into the sky.

CHAPTER 8

Aang looked down at the Northern Air Temple as Appa circled the ancient structure from above. The temple rested atop a series of tall stone columns that rose up from a canyon below. A metal bridge, obviously made by the Fire Nation, extended from one side of the temple, stretching across the canyon to a stone landing just beyond the columns.

"That Fire Nation bridge gives me the creeps, Appa," Aang said as they swooped down into the temple's courtyard. "It certainly wasn't here the last time I visited this place."

Appa landed. Aang slid off the bison's back and slowly made his way into the temple. Walking down a long hallway, he spotted a figure standing at the far end of the hall.

"I didn't know anyone would be here," Aang said as the figure walked toward him.

Stepping into a pool of light, the figure revealed himself to be an old man with a wrinkled smile. "Who are you?" the old man asked.

Aang removed his hood, revealing his tattoos.

"It cannot be!" the man cried, staring at Aang in disbelief. "I heard stories, but . . . are you . . . ?"

Aang nodded. "My name is Aang," he said.

The old man shook his head. "I cannot believe I have lived to see your return," he said weakly.

Aang glanced around the interior of the temple. The walls were burned and crumbling, the ceilings scarred and cracked. The once-grand temple was in a shambles. "The Fire Nation destroyed this temple," Aang said, anger flashing in his eyes. "They have ruined everything."

"Not everything," the old man said. "I live near here. I have visited many times. There is a hidden chamber of statues I think you, of all people, should see."

The old man led Aang into a huge room with a tall, arched ceiling. The room was filled with hundreds of life-size statues, each one a representation of a different person. Half were men, half were women. Aang immediately recognized the next-to-last statue as that of Avatar Kyoshi, wrapped in her kimono, holding her fan. He did not recognize the last statue in line, which stood next to Avatar Kyoshi's. It was of a tall, handsome man dressed in Fire Nation clothing.

"These are all the past Avatars," the old man said,

gesturing to the room full of statues. "These are the reincarnations of you over the years." Then he pointed to the last one in the line, the tall man in the Fire Nation outfit. "Avatar Roku was your last life."

Aang stared up at the statue. He knew the cycle of Avatar rebirth went from Air to Water to Earth to Fire, then back to Air. He realized that the Avatar before him would have been from the Fire Nation, but seeing the image of Avatar Roku for the first time moved him more than he expected. He grew very curious about the man who had preceded him.

"How did the airbenders know you were the Avatar, little one?" the old man asked, interrupting Aang's thoughts.

"They gave me a test," Aang explained, his thoughts now turning to his days with the monks at the Southern Air Temple. "They put a thousand toys in front of me and asked me to choose four. They said I chose the same four toys the previous Avatars played with when they were children."

He thought about when the monks told him he was the Avatar, and then thought about what had caused him to run away on that very day. The burden of his great responsibility suddenly overwhelmed him again.

"That same day they told me I could have no family," Aang continued. "They told me my responsibility to the four nations would have to be my main focus and the most important thing in my life."

The old man looked at Aang. "You seem like a nice young man," he said. "You really do. You will forgive me, won't you?"

"For what?" Aang asked, not understanding.

"For luring you down here," the old man said softly. "I have lived in poverty because of your absence, Avatar, so you will understand my actions today."

Before Aang could say a word, the old man pulled out a knife and flashed the blade at Aang, who immediately heard the sound of many feet scraping against the stone floor of the room. Looking up, Aang saw hundreds of Fire Nation soldiers stepping out from behind the Avatar statues. Each soldier gripped a bow, loaded with an arrow, tensed and ready to fire.

Aang watched in shock as the old man slipped away from him and backed into the shadows, a guilty look on his face. There, the old man extended his hand and took several coins from a Fire Nation soldier, his payment for betraying the Avatar. Then the old man hurried from the room.

Aang looked all around. Hundreds of arrows were pointed right at him. He thought for a moment about bounding into the air, unleashing an airbending blast, and trying to escape. But there were just too many soldiers. Even he could not move fast enough to avoid all those arrows.

Aang dropped his head in resignation. A soldier came forward, roughly bound Aang's wrists, and led him from the room.

Back at their campsite, Sokka and Katara gathered wood for that evening's fire. Katara looked out over the lake in the direction Aang had flown the night before.

"Do you think something's wrong?" she asked Sokka, who stood clutching an armful of firewood and staring into the forest.

"Katara," he whispered urgently, nodding his head toward the woods behind her.

Katara spun around and saw a squad of Fire Nation soldiers, marching out of the woods. She instinctively reached for the water pouch that usually hung from her waist. It wasn't there. She glanced over to their campsite and spotted both her water pouch and Sokka's boomerang lying on the ground at the base of a nearby tree.

Within seconds Katara and Sokka were surrounded by Fire Nation soldiers. Two soldiers pushed a metal cart filled with burning wood embers. Three black-clad firebenders stepped to the front of the group and raised their arms to shoulder level. Flames shot upward from the embers, flickering above the cart.

"Kill them!" boomed a voice from the Fire Nation squad leader.

Sokka and Katara turned and looked at each other, their eyes opened wide in fear. There was nowhere to run. They had no weapons with which to defend themselves. And Aang was not there to protect them. They were doomed and they knew it.

"Katara, I love you," Sokka said softly.

"I love you too," Katara replied, her voice choked with emotion.

The firebenders thrust their hands forward in a move designed to direct a blast of fire right at the brother and sister. But before they completed their move, a spinning metal fan flew through the air from above, slamming into one of the firebenders and knocking him to the ground.

The remaining soldiers looked up, along with Sokka and Katara, just in time to see several figures clad in green kimonos leap from the forest trees. They landed behind the firebenders, who turned to confront them.

Taking advantage of the distraction, Sokka and Katara dashed to the campsite. Katara grabbed her water pouch and opened it. Sokka snatched up his boomerang, struck a warrior's pose, and let out a piercing battle cry.

"Yiiiiiiii!" he shrieked, but the powerful yell quickly dwindled to a confused moan. "Huh?"

Sokka and Katara both stared in shock at the scene before them. The battle was over. A dozen Fire Nation soldiers and firebenders lay sprawled on the ground, unconscious. Standing over them were the figures who had jumped from the trees, several female warriors. Their long hair flowed down onto their green kimonos, and their beautiful faces were painted white. Each held a metal fan. The warriors stepped forward, then stared at Sokka and Katara.

"I am Suki," the warrior closest to Sokka announced.

"I'm the leader of the Kyoshi warriors. Our order has been fighting the Fire Nation for decades. We have heard word of the Avatar's existence and have been shadowing you."

Sokka lowered his boomerang and looked over at Katara, his eyebrows raised.

"We offer our services to protect the Avatar until he reaches the northernmost border of the Earth Kingdom," Suki continued. "From there we will leave you and return to fight in the growing rebellion. Your leader's idea of spreading news of the Avatar throughout the villages is working. The Fire Nation does not know how to fight such an infection of spirit. Thank your leader for us."

"That was my idea, actually," Sokka said, beaming with pride.

"Where is the Avatar?" Suki asked.

"He needed to do something. If we wait here, he'll come back very soon," Katara replied, looking out over the lake, her expression changing to one of great concern. I hope, she thought.

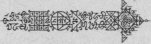

Now a Fire Nation prisoner, Aang was hanging from chains in a prayer room in the Northern Air Temple. For the past hour he had been going in and out of consciousness. He could feel himself drifting into that strange meditative state once again.

A thick white mist overtook him. He was again walking

"The Fire Nation is here. And they brought their war machines."

"I'm taking you to my ship. If you don't come, I'll burn down this village."

"We have to save him!"

"You found the Avatar. Your destinies are tied, Zuko."

"This belonged to Monk Gyatso. I made it for him."

"Aang, I think you were in that ice for a hundred years. The Fire Nation started a war."

"To master water, you must release your emotions, wherever they may lead you."

"I am the Avatar."

"The Fire Nation is here!"

"Take me to the spiritual place!"

The Avatar has mastered water!

through a shrouded forest. This time he knew for certain that he had reentered the spirit world.

He soon came to the familiar cave. Stepping in he saw the Dragon's snakelike body slithering across the damp cave floor. Then he heard the Dragon's deep voice fill the cave.

"There are the seeds of belief among the Fire Nation that the spirit world's time of influence over the humans should end," the Dragon said. Then the beast's enormous head poked through the thick mist and drew close to Aang. Thick, scaly skin covered its face. Long, sharp teeth filled its mouth.

"The Fire Nation has stolen secret knowledge of the spirit world from the Great Library," the Dragon continued. "They are intending to misuse this knowledge."

Aang took a deep breath and tried to summon his courage. "I will stop them," he stated firmly.

A huge dragon claw appeared suddenly from the mist. The Dragon pondered Aang's words.

"I know you will try," the Dragon said after a moment. "But it requires many, many years to master all the elements. The comet that gave the Fire Nation the power to start this war one hundred years ago will be returning in three years. It will once again give the firebenders the ability to use their chi to produce fire themselves, rather than just manipulate already existing fire. Every firebender will be able to create fire and use it against their enemies. If they have not been defeated by the day the comet returns, nothing will be able to stop them."

This news hit Aang hard. His fear of not being good enough, of not having enough time to learn all he needed to learn, came crashing back down on him.

"Spirits can sense things about the future," Aang said, pushing back the wave of emotion that threatened to overtake him. "Will I stop them? Will I fix everything?"

"I don't know, Avatar Aang," the Dragon replied. "It is unclear."

"Can you tell me anything of the future?" Aang asked, practically pleading with the Dragon for some shred of hope.

"I can tell you that the one called Katara will be very important to you," the Dragon said. "But be careful with your feelings and actions. You have struggled with this in all of your lifetimes, Avatar: the balance between your desire for love and family, and your responsibility to the world. You have begun to change things, but now you must get to the Northern Water Tribe. The Fire Nation will soon attack, and they have information that can help them defeat the Water Tribe. If they succeed there, all is lost."

"But what—," Aang began to speak, but the Dragon vanished into the cloud of mist, which filled the cave, completely engulfing Aang.

CHAPTER 9

Aang's eyes opened slowly. He realized he was no longer in the spirit world cave. Instead he could see that he was still dangling from the chain in the Northern Air Temple's prayer room. Lifting his head, Aang saw a tall, muscular man with a fierce-looking face and deep, brown eyes standing before him. The man wore a Fire Nation army uniform.

"Wake up," the tall man said. "My name is Commander Zhao. I set this trap for you. Don't worry, I will not kill you. You would just be reborn, and my search would continue. Where have you been for all this time? And how is it you are still a boy?"

Aang just stared at the man. He had no intention of giving this Fire Nation commander any information.

Zhao continued his interrogation. "I understand when you

freed that handful of towns you were quite impressive, but you only used airbending against my soldiers. Why is that?"

Again Aang remained silent. Zhao reached down and slid a large bucket of water directly under Aang's dangling feet. "You know," Zhao said almost playfully, "I hate water. I don't even know how to swim."

Aang stared down at the bucket.

"Well, what are you waiting for? Use that water. Go ahead, bend it. I'm defenseless."

Aang still didn't move, confirming Zhao's suspicions.

"As I thought," the Fire Nation commander muttered.

Aang turned his head away.

"I wish I was there when the comet came and they killed the rest of your kind," Zhao said, with a sharp, cruel edge in his voice. "I hear the airbenders were very cowardly. They didn't even fight. Did you know that? Sad, really."

Aang felt flushed with shame. Zhao was right. He should have been there. He should have saved his people.

"I am disappointed, though," Zhao said, after allowing Aang a long moment to wallow in guilt and pain. "I thought I would be a little more impressed when I finally caught you." Then he strode from the room, slamming the door loudly behind him.

A dark figure crouched in the shadows at the entrance to the bridge leading from the canyon to the Northern Air

Temple. He watched as a huge Fire Nation military machine rolled up to the entrance, paused as the driver spoke with a guard who waved him through, then proceeded out onto the bridge. Moving with blinding quickness, the figure slipped under the rolling machine and grabbed onto its undercarriage, hitching a ride.

When the machine reached the temple, the dark figure let go and silently dropped to the ground. He scrambled to the temple and slipped inside, unnoticed.

In the passageway leading to the prayer room, the dark figure encountered several Fire Nation guards.

"Stop, who are you?" one guard shouted, startled by the black-clad figure in the blue mask.

The masked figure did not reply. Nor did he stop. He thrust his arms forward, wielding his swords with skill and grace. With speed and agility, he quickly took down each guard, clearing the passageway.

The dark figure reached the prayer room and stepped inside, closing the door behind him. He saw Aang dangling from the ceiling.

Aang stared at the stranger's terrifying blue mask that had been painted with a broad evil grin. He tensed up immediately.

"Who are you?" he asked.

The blue-masked figure reached behind his back and pulled two gleaming silver swords out of their scabbards.

"Wait! Don't!" Aang cried, feeling more helpless than he ever had before.

The figure raised his swords. Aang closed his eyes. The swords whirled and slashed, slicing through the chains that bound Aang. He dropped to the ground, free from his bondage. Aang rubbed his wrists and stared at the mysterious figure who had just freed him.

The blue-masked stranger opened the door and nodded his head toward the doorway. Then he slipped out into the passageway. Aang snatched up his staff and followed. As they moved silently down the corridor, Aang observed the unconscious Fire Nation guards that his rescuer had left behind on his way into the prayer room.

Suddenly the stranger stopped short and pushed Aang into a dark corner. The two pressed their backs against the wall and watched as Commander Zhao and his assistant arrived at the prayer room.

"Send word to the Fire Lord that once again I have accomplished what he asked me to do without incident—" Zhao stopped short at the sight of the fallen Fire Nation guards. He threw open the door to the prayer room, only to discover that it was now empty.

"Incompetent fools," he muttered.

Just then a Fire Nation soldier rushed up to Zhao. "Sir," the soldier began. "The troops are reporting seeing a strange, blue-faced intruder. They are calling him the Blue Spirit."

Zhao turned to his assistant. "Order the gates closed. The Avatar has escaped. We must seal him and this Blue Spirit inside."

Aang and the Blue Spirit raced toward the temple courtyard. Two soldiers stepped into their path.

"I've got this," Aang said, unleashing a powerful air-bending blast that knocked the soldiers away.

Reaching the courtyard, Aang and the Blue Spirit found themselves surrounded by many Fire Nation soldiers. The men rushed at them, forcing Aang to dash toward one side of the courtyard and the Blue Spirit to head in the opposite direction.

As he approached the edge of the courtyard, four fire-benders surrounded the blue-masked figure.

"Let's see how you handle fire, Blue Spirit!" one of the firebenders shouted.

Then, moving as one, the four firebenders pulled fire from burning pots stationed all around the courtyard and flung the searing flames at the Blue Spirit.

Moving with almost supernatural speed, the Blue Spirit reached back and snatched his silver swords, deflecting the fire blasts away with his lightning-quick blades.

Across the courtyard, Aang stopped before a row of giant conch shells. A squad of Fire Nation soldiers quickly surrounded him. Following a set of markings on the ground, Aang went through a series of classic airbending moves, thrusting his hands toward the enormous shells.

A huge blast of air shot through the shells, amplified by their shape. The air exploded out the other end, sending the soldiers skidding back across the courtyard. Aang repeated this move again and again, using these weapons of his ancestors as only he, the Last Airbender, could.

When he had blasted all the soldiers, Aang lowered his hands and looked around. "This was their practice area," he muttered.

Aang turned and started running, leaping out of the courtyard and jumping from one stone column to another, making his way across the canyon. His anger grew as he thought about what the Fire Nation had done to this once-great temple.

Opening the wings on his staff and preparing to leave the canyon behind, Aang glanced back over his shoulder. He spotted the Blue Spirit down in the courtyard, battling a group of firebenders. Aang could have simply taken to the air and flown away, returning to Katara and Sokka and continuing on his journey to the Northern Water Tribe. But whoever this person behind the mask was, he had rescued Aang. Without his help, Aang would still have been a prisoner of the Fire Nation.

He snapped his staff shut, turned around, and ran back, column by column, until he got to the courtyard. Landing beside the Blue Spirit, Aang stepped forward and rotated his hands, sending an airbending blast right into a group of soldiers who were about to attack his masked comrade.

Returning the favor, the Blue Spirit dove and blocked two blasts of fire that were about to strike Aang. Though they fought fiercely, the duo was vastly outnumbered.

Several firebenders began to execute a group move designed to take out the two prisoners for good.

"Do not kill the Avatar," a voice boomed from the back of the group of firebenders. They stopped their move, mid-form. Commander Zhao pushed his way to the front of the soldiers. "He will just be reborn again." The fighting stopped for a moment as Zhao stared at the two combatants.

Then suddenly the Blue Spirit turned and grabbed Aang from behind, placing one of his swords to the boy's throat. Aang's eyes went wide with fear and confusion.

Commander Zhao stared at the Blue Spirit. "Why are you doing this?" Zhao asked. "Who are you?"

The two stared at each other intensely. Zhao peered into the eye holes of the blue mask, locking eyes with the figure behind the frightening image. A look of recognition spread across Zhao's face.

The Blue Spirit gestured to the gates leading to the bridge out of the courtyard.

"Open the gates," Zhao ordered. "Let them out."

His soldiers hesitated for a moment, but soon hurried to open the gates. The Blue Spirit, his blade still pressed against Aang's throat, slowly backed away and crossed the bridge. When they reached the land on the other side of the canyon, the Blue Spirit quickened his pace, although he kept his sword firmly on Aang's throat.

Aang heard a high-pitched whistling sound coming from the direction of the temple. He looked back in time to see an arrow slice through the air and strike his captor directly in the mask.

The Blue Spirit went down, hitting the ground hard. He lay there unconscious, his mask split in two. Looking back at the temple, Aang spotted Zhao standing on a high balcony beside an archer who held an empty bow.

Aang turned back to the fallen figure. "Are you okay?" he asked.

The Blue Spirit remained motionless. Then, reaching down, Aang removed the pieces of the mask. He fell back in shock at the sight before him. Aang was staring down into the face of Prince Zuko.

CHAPTER 10

Aang's mind was a mess of confusion. Zuko? Aang thought. Did he rescue me just so he could capture me himself?

Aang looked back at the temple and saw Fire Nation soldiers hurrying over the bridge to chase after them. He looked into the sky and spotted a group of passing clouds. He planted his feet firmly and shoved his hands forward, palms outward, in an airbending move. The cloud descended, reaching ground level in a few seconds, covering the charging soldiers, Aang, and Zuko in a thick, white fog. Aang picked up Zuko, slung him over his shoulder, and made for the forest as fast as he could run.

A short while later the sun began to set. Aang found a spot to camp for the night. He built a campfire and sat beside the still-unconscious form of Zuko, pondering his next move.

He had to get back to Katara and Sokka, and he couldn't lose any more time in getting to the Northern Water Tribe. But he also knew he couldn't just leave Zuko there.

Aang sat by the fire through the night, adding wood to keep them both warm. Glancing at Zuko, he noticed something peeking out of the prince's pocket. Pulling it out, Aang saw that it was Katara's Water Tribe necklace. He smiled, then slipped it into his own pocket. He had no idea how Zuko had gotten it, but he was glad to have discovered it. Katara would be so happy to get it back.

Zuko rose with the sun, groaning and forcing his eyes open. The moment he spotted Aang, he struggled to his feet. With a swift firebending move, Zuko pulled from the glowing embers of the campfire and hurtled three spikes of blazing orange flames at Aang.

Aang leaped to a nearby tree, jumping from branch to branch, to avoid Zuko's relentless firebending barrage. He rescued me and then I rescued him, Aang thought as he climbed higher and disappeared into the thick forest canopy. I guess we're even.

Commander Zhao stood stiffly in the vast royal hall of the Fire Lord's palace. Nearby, the Fire Lord paced across the gleaming marble floor. Intricate metal carvings ran up the walls, cresting in the high arched ceiling. Woven banners, depicting glorious Fire Nation battles, hung around the hall.

"Commander Zhao, how was your trip?" the Fire Lord asked, his tone pleasant.

Zhao fidgeted nervously, but said nothing.

"How did he escape?" the Fire Lord asked, as if reading Zhao's mind, his tone much more serious now.

Zhao swallowed hard, then launched into the speech he had prepared on the journey home. "I fear that your son is not only incompetent, but he is also a traitor. Of course, I cannot prove that, sire."

The Fire Lord stopped pacing and looked at Zhao. "You think my son was this person the soldiers are calling the Blue Spirit?" he asked flatly.

"Yes," Zhao replied, feeling slightly less anxious.

"If my son is a traitor, then there is nothing left to speak of," the Fire Lord said. "Take care of this for me, Zhao, but do not make it look like I had anything to do with it. Make it appear to be an accident. An unfortunate accident."

"I understand, sire," Zhao said quickly. "And I'm sorry about your son."

"And what of the Avatar?" the Fire Lord asked, quickly changing the subject.

"It has been confirmed that he is traveling north," Zhao explained. "There have been sightings of him at the northernmost edges of the Earth Kingdom. It is my strong belief that he is traveling to the Northern Water Tribe."

The Fire Lord glanced at Zhao, unable to hide his surprise at this news.

"Why is that, Commander?" the Fire Lord asked.

"I believe this child Avatar has knowledge of only his birth element, Air," Zhao replied. "I believe he is trying to learn the discipline of Water. He has gone to seek out a teacher in the Northern Water Tribe, where they have lived beyond our reach and openly practiced waterbending."

Fire Lord Ozai thought about this for a moment. Then he spoke. "This is good news, indeed. Perhaps this child is not as powerful as we had feared."

"My thoughts exactly, sire," Zhao replied. "I will travel to the Northern Water Tribe city and end this threat."

Fire Lord Ozai raised a hand, his expression turning stern. "Do not underestimate the power of the Northern Water Tribe, Commander," he said. "They are given their strength by the Moon and Ocean Spirits. It will be difficult to beat them."

Zhao waited patiently, eager to hear the plan that was forming in the Fire Lord's mind.

"Now, if for some reason the spirits weren't involved," the Fire Lord continued, "that, of course, would change everything. What have you learned from the scrolls you stole from the Great Library?"

This was the moment Zhao had been waiting for. He had information he had been saving for just such a time. "We have deciphered the location of the Moon and Ocean Spirits," Zhao announced proudly.

The Fire Lord smiled for the first time. "It is our destiny to have found this information, Zhao," he said.

Zhao nodded his agreement. "If we take the Northern Water Tribe, it could tip the war in our favor," he said. "And our knowledge of their spirits is the way to compromise the city."

"We no longer need to cower before the spirits like some primitive people," the Fire Lord said defiantly. "Eliminate the spirits, Zhao. Take the city and destroy the Avatar at the same time."

Prince Zuko stumbled through the woods. Although still battered and bruised from his adventure as the Blue Spirit, harder to swallow was the bitter disappointment of losing the Avatar when he had him right in his grasp. For the second time. Emerging from the thick woods, Zuko found his uncle by the riverbank.

"Zhao's men have been searching the coast, looking for you," Iroh said at the sight of his nephew. "I told them you went on vacation with a girl. They were on your ship, searching it. Where have you been for four days, Zuko?"

"Nowhere," the prince muttered, heading for his ship which was docked on the river. Just before he stepped onboard, Zuko turned to his uncle. "We have to keep moving. The Avatar is traveling again."

"Take rest first," Iroh suggested. "It looks like you've been through a great deal. When you wake, we'll have tea together and set out on our way."

Zuko nodded and headed onto the ship. Reaching his quarters, he stretched out on his cot and closed his eyes, hoping to take his uncle's advice and get some rest before continuing his pursuit of the Avatar.

But something was wrong. Zuko immediately heard something hissing near the torch on his wall. Bounding from his bed, Zuko dashed from his quarters and ran across the deck, desperately trying to get off the ship before—

KA-THOOM!

Iroh watched in horror from the shore as Zuko's ship exploded into a huge, orange fireball.

"Zuko!" he cried as flames completely engulfed the ship.

CHAPTER 11

Katara paced back and forth at the edge of the lake, stopping every few seconds to look up. Sokka sat nearby, tossing rocks into the water.

"We've got to do something," Katara blurted.

"Katara, we've been over this again and again," Sokka replied. "We don't even know where this temple is. There's nothing to do but wait. He can take care of himself. He'll be back. Just be patient, like them." Sokka tilted his head in the direction of the Kyoshi warriors, who were sitting quietly and meditating.

A few more minutes passed when suddenly a large shadow fell over Katara.

"Aang!" she cried, as she looked up and spotted Appa.

Appa landed. Aang slid off his back, bowed to the Kyoshi

warriors, then joined Sokka and Katara in a group hug.

"We were so worried about you," Katara cried.

"I'm okay," Aang explained as the group dispersed. "I was captured at the Northern Air Temple, but I got some help from an unexpected person." Aang then told his friends the tale of how Zuko, dressed as the Blue Spirit, first rescued him, then tried to capture him.

"Which reminds me," Aang said as he finished his story. "I have something for you, Katara." He reached into his pocket, pulled out her necklace, and placed it gently around her neck. Their eyes locked for a moment as both felt the joy and relief of seeing each other again.

"We'd better keep moving," Aang said after a moment. "We've got to get to the Northern Water Tribe."

Katara, Sokka, and Aang climbed up onto Appa's back.

"We will follow you on the ground and make sure your way is free from Fire Nation interference," Suki said.

"Thank you," Aang said. "I'm sure Avatar Kyoshi would be proud of you." Then he bowed toward them, slipped on his hooded cloak, and shouted, "Appa, yip-yip!"

Appa took off into the sky.

"They've been following us for miles," Sokka announced anxiously to Katara and Aang, motioning toward the band of Fire Nation soldiers on their tail.

The group had been traveling for a few hours when they

finally approached the northern border of the Earth Kingdom. Looking down, Sokka had spotted a troop of twenty Fire Nation soldiers, running on the road below. Then he saw a group of women standing in the middle of the road, trying to push an overturned cart back onto its wheels. Blocked by this obstacle, the Fire Nation soldiers slowed to a stop.

"Get out of the road," the lead soldier ordered. "You are interfering with official Fire Nation business."

"We could use the help of some strong soldiers, sir," said one of the women weakly.

As the troops reached the overturned cart, the women turned around, revealing their white painted faces.

"It's Suki and the other Kyoshi warriors!" Sokka cried. "They've set a trap."

The Kyoshi warriors pulled metal fans from beneath their cloaks and attacked. Within a few moments they had defeated the stunned Fire Nation soldiers.

Aang and his friends continued on their way. Soon, lush green mountains gave way to snow-covered hills. The white mountains led to a vast ocean. Blue-tinted glaciers jutted up from the water as Appa splashed down into the icy sea. The bison used his flat, paddle-shaped tail to propel himself through the water, swimming around glaciers and past icebergs. Sokka searched his maps, trying to figure out exactly where they were.

"Look!" Katara shouted suddenly. "Men in boats. And they're wearing Water Tribe clothing. Sokka, we're here. We've found the Northern Water Tribe!"

CHAPTER 12

"Over here!" Sokka and Katara shouted together, waving their arms frantically.

The men of the Water Tribe paddled their boat over to Appa. Their eyes opened wide in surprise at the sight of the enormous floating bison. Sokka and Katara smiled broadly. They had never met their brothers from the Northern Water Tribe, though their father had told them stories of the powerful benders there. Aang remained silent and hooded.

"I am a waterbender from the Southern Water Tribe," Katara announced. "And I travel with a person of great importance."

Sokka beamed with pride. He had no idea that his sister considered him a person of great importance. Then he sighed and his shoulders slumped as he realized that Katara was referring to Aang.

"We must see your princess and your finest waterbending masters," Katara added.

The men of the Northern Water Tribe nodded. "Follow us back to the stronghold," one of them said.

A few minutes later Aang peered out from under his hood to see a stronghold formed from huge walls of ice that rose up from the ocean's surface. A narrow channel created a small opening in the walls. Appa followed the Water Tribe boats through this channel and into the stronghold.

Aang, Sokka, and Katara stepped off Appa and followed the men, who had led them across the main courtyard of the Northern Water Tribe stronghold. Crowds formed as they moved across the vast icy plaza, staring at the enormous fur-covered beast and the strangers he had carried to their home.

The Water Tribe men led the visitors into a glistening crystal palace of ice. They were brought to a large chamber where they stood before a group of the tribe's leaders. In the center of the group sat a beautiful sixteen-year-old girl with long white hair and deep, soulful eyes. Sokka found himself immediately lost in the girl's eyes—until she noticed him staring at her, and looked away. Then she stood and spoke to the newcomers.

"I am Princess Yue, and I welcome you to the Northern Water Tribe," she said.

"I am Katara, a waterbender from the Southern Water Tribe," Katara began, realizing that everyone was staring at her. She noticed one older man who sat alone in the corner and stared at her with particular intensity. "This is my brother, Sokka, a warrior from the Southern Water Tribe."

Sokka bowed, and Katara continued, telling the group of their long journey from the South Pole through the Earth Kingdom, and all the way here to find their sister tribe.

Then she paused and turned to Aang.

"We welcome our brethren from the south," one of the elders said. "But who is this other young one? He does not dress like a Water tribesman."

Aang took off his cloak and exposed his airbending tattoos. He performed a simple airbending move, creating a spinning funnel of air in the chamber. Everyone in the room stood up. A flurry of mutterings sped through the room. They could not believe their eyes.

"The Avatar?"

"He has returned?"

"There is hope!"

"Where has he been?"

Katara raised her hands to quiet the chattering group. "The Avatar needs to learn waterbending from your finest master," she explained as the group fell silent. "Is there one here among you who can teach him?"

All eyes immediately turned to the old man in the corner. He stood slowly.

"I am Master Pakku," he said in a surprisingly strong voice for one who looked so frail. "And I will teach the Avatar!"

Following a feast in honor of the Avatar's return—and the first good night's sleep Aang and his friends had had in many weeks—Aang began his waterbending training with Master Pakku. Not wanting to miss out on this once-in-a-lifetime chance, Katara also joined in the training class, hoping to improve her own skills. During the course of the many weeks that followed, they learned classic forms, practiced drills, and engaged in sparring matches.

"Water is what?" Master Pakku asked as the day's lessons began.

"The flowing element. The element of change," the entire class recited together.

"Correct," Master Pakku said. "To master Water, you must release your emotions, wherever they may lead you. Water teaches us acceptance. Let your emotions flow like Water." Then he turned to Aang. "Aang, would you like to spar? You haven't sparred in a few days."

Aang nodded, then stepped forward. He and his teacher faced each other, brought their hands together, and bowed. The sparring match had begun.

Master Pakku wasted no time in striking first. He lifted his arms into the air, causing bars of ice to rise from the frozen ground, forming a prison all around Aang. Aang immediately placed his hands on the ground and bent the ice bars away from himself, opening the cage.

As Aang stepped free, Master Pakku flung four balls of water at him. Standing his ground, Aang raised his hands and spread his fingers apart. The water balls stopped right in front of him and broke into hundreds of tiny drops, splashing to the ground at his feet.

"Two excellent defensive maneuvers," Master Pakku said. "Now use offense, Aang."

Aang raised his hands swiftly and lifted a two-foot wave of water from a nearby canal. As the mass of water hung in the air quivering, all the canals that ran through the stronghold began to bubble and churn. Master Pakku and his students looked around at the vibrating canals, which began to rise above their banks.

Everyone turned and stared at Aang in awe—and also with a bit of fear. The extent of Aang's power was astounding. The mass of water splashed to the ground, and the canals became still once again. He slowly brought his hands together and bowed before his teacher. As the lesson ended, Aang realized that despite his great power, he still had so much to learn if he was going to truly take his place as the Avatar.

While Aang and Katara trained with Master Pakku during their many weeks at the Northern Water Tribe stronghold, Sokka spent most of his time with Princess Yue.

"I've loved spending these weeks with you, Sokka," the

princess whispered as the couple strolled through the ice city.

"Me too," Sokka replied, gently taking Yue's hand into his own. During their time together, he had developed deep feelings for the princess, unlike anything he had ever felt before.

"Should we see what the ocean is doing today?" Yue asked.

Sokka nodded and smiled. The couple headed up a staircase leading to the top of the enormous wall that protected the stronghold from the power of the open ocean. Looking back, they had a breathtaking view of the entire city. The ocean stretched for what seemed like forever in a rolling carpet of whitecapped blue.

"When there is some safety for all of us, I will come visit our sister city in the Southern Water Tribe and spend time in your home," Yue said, looking right into Sokka's eyes.

"That would be great," he replied enthusiastically. "But I warn you, my grandmother will ask you a lot of questions."

"What might she ask me?" Yue inquired, tilting her head and raising her eyebrows.

Sokka thought for moment. "She'll say, 'Why is your hair white, young lady? You look very odd.'"

"I would say to your grandmother, 'My hair is white because when I was born, I was not awake. My mother and father could not get me to make a sound or move. They prayed for days to the Moon Spirit, then they dipped me in the sacred waters. My parents said it was then that my hair turned white, and life poured into me. The Moon Spirit gave me life.'"

Sokka stared at Yue, his eyes and mouth opened wide. "Wow," he cried. "You didn't tell me that."

"You didn't ask me," Yue replied. "Only your grandmother did."

"She might ask another question, too," Sokka said immediately.

"What?" Yue asked, enjoying this little game.

"She might ask what your feelings are for her grandson," Sokka prodded.

"I would tell her," Yue began, her eyes never leaving Sokka's eyes, "that I think I found my best friend in her grandson."

Sokka squeezed Yue's hand tightly and sighed. Glancing down into the courtyard below, he saw Aang and Katara practicing waterbending forms, long after the rest of their class had gone home. Sokka realized it had been a long while since he had thought about the great danger the world faced or the difficult task that lay before them. For the first time in a very long time, he was happy. Genuinely happy.

Turing back to the ocean, he noticed what appeared to be black snow drifting gently down from the sky.

Princess Yue held out her hand and caught one of the flakes, which smudged into ash on her palm. "What is this?" she asked anxiously.

Sokka turned to face her. "Yue," he said as thoughts of the great dangers he had managed to shove aside came flooding back into his mind, "the Fire Nation is here."

CHAPTER 13

Commander Zhao stood on the deck of his warship, peering out at the icy ocean as the Northern Water Tribe stronghold came into view. His thoughts of capturing the Avatar and crushing the growing rebellion against the Fire Nation were interrupted by the sound of someone joining him on deck.

"General Iroh," Zhao said, turning to greet his guest. "I'm glad you accepted my invitation to join us at this historic event."

Iroh bowed slightly. "Your invitation was very gracious," he replied.

"You are a gifted strategist," Zhao continued. "No one can argue that. Your failure in the Hundred Day Siege of Ba Sing Se won't be held against you." He paused for a moment to allow the memory of Iroh's greatest defeat to return to his mind. Then he went on. "Your son died in that siege, didn't he?"

"Yes, he did," Iroh replied, his voice and face betraying no emotion.

"And again, let me offer my condolences on your nephew burning to death in that terrible accident on his ship," Zhao added solemnly.

"Thank you," Iroh said. "I'm sure my brother, the Fire Lord, was very upset at the loss of his own son." Then he bowed and strode from the deck.

On a lower level of the ship, Iroh moved down a darkened hallway, walked past two guards who saluted him, then slipped into a storage room, carefully closing the door behind him.

There he found a guard in a uniform and helmet, searching through boxes. The guard turned and removed his helmet, revealing himself to be Prince Zuko in disguise. Zuko had managed to dive off his ship, just as it exploded, and so survived the blast. When Iroh accepted Zhao's invitation to come to the Northern Water Tribe stronghold, he snuck his nephew onboard.

"Any problems?" Zuko asked.

"We have arrived at the Northern Water Tribe stronghold," Iroh explained, shaking his head. "They believe the boy is there."

"Why do you seem upset, Uncle?" Zuko asked.

"Zhao has no sacredness," Iroh replied. "He is cold-blooded and insincere. He believes that you died on your boat, and he thinks that I believe it was an accident. Are you sure you want to be here?"

Zuko stared hard at his uncle. "I will not be allowed to live in peace by Zhao or anyone else until I bring the Avatar to my father," Zuko said fiercely. "Is that still not clear to you?"

"Very well, Prince Zuko," Iroh said, sighing. "Stay quiet and remain hidden." Then he left the storage room, closing the door carefully behind him.

Arriving at the ship's war council room, Iroh found Commander Zhao poring over maps. His guards stood nearby, alert. "Ah, General, come in," Zhao said when Iroh appeared at the door.

"The waterbenders get power from the moon," Iroh began. "They will get stronger as the day comes to an end."

"General Iroh, I have been keeping a secret," Zhao said in response.

"What is that?" Iroh asked suspiciously.

"In my raid of the Great Library earlier this year, I found a scroll that tells the location of the Ocean and Moon Spirits," Zhao said triumphantly.

Iroh stepped back, genuinely shocked. "The Ocean and Moon Spirits?" he repeated.

"You seem excited by this news," Zhao said, gauging Iroh's reaction.

Iroh composed himself before responding. "To meet a spirit would be a great honor," he said.

Zhao chuckled to himself. "Well, I hope I can give you that honor."

Iroh nodded, then left the war council room.

A short time later Iroh along with Zuko slipped from the storage room and snuck up to the deck at the rear of the ship.

"Be sure to keep your uniform closed up to your neck," Iroh said. "Your own chi and firebending ability can warm you in the icy ocean. And remember to change your wet clothes when you get out of the water."

Zuko nodded. "I will remember," he said, fastening the top button of his uniform.

As Zuko moved closer to the edge of the deck, Iroh cried out in a voice choked with emotion. "Zuko!"

The prince paused and looked back at his uncle, who was fighting back tears.

"You have always been like a son to me," Iroh said.

Zuko smiled. "I know, Uncle," he said softly. Then he jumped into a small boat and steered it toward the Northern Water Tribe's outer wall. As he neared the shores of the stronghold, Zuko took a deep breath, then dove beneath the water's surface, propelling himself down and forward. He saw nothing but darkness ahead of him. Glancing back up, he saw a thick layer of ice above him with no obvious way back to the surface.

The freezing cold water gripped his face. Panic set in. Zuko was lost beneath the ice, and running out of air. He remembered his uncle's words and calmed himself, knowing it would conserve what little air he had left.

Floating up to the surface, Zuko placed the palms of his hands on the underside of the ice. Focusing his firebending energy, his hands began to glow red, and the ice began to melt. He started to slowly rise through the ice. When he had finally managed to burn a hole completely through the ice, Zuko emerged, gasping for breath, pulling himself up out of the water and rolling onto the surface of the ice.

Scrambling to his feet, Zuko saw that he was inside the igloolike home of a member of the Northern Water Tribe. Firebending small amounts of heat, Zuko warmed his entire body. Then he slipped from the home and dashed out into the stronghold.

Warning bells blared throughout the stronghold. The people of the tribe rushed from their homes, knowing that something was terribly wrong. A crowd quickly gathered in the courtyard, and a steady stream of people raced up the stairs to the top of the stronghold's outer wall.

One by one they reached the top. And one by one they turned pale, their hearts gripped with fear at the sight of a massive fleet of Fire Nation warships lined up in the water just beyond the wall. They could stay hidden no more. Tonight they would fight for their lives.

CHAPTER 14

Aang, Katara, Sokka, and Princess Yue stood on the balcony of Yue's home, looking out at the armada of Fire Nation ships. Aang and Sokka huddled on one side of the long terrace; Katara and the princess stood together on the other end.

"You are very close to the Avatar, aren't you?" Yue asked Katara softly.

"We're close friends," Katara replied without taking her eyes from the horrifying sight just beyond the stronghold wall.

"It's good that we have become a family," the princess said. "We will need one another."

Aang and Sokka walked up next to the girls.

"Aang needs to ask you something," Sokka said to Yue, placing a gentle hand on her shoulder.

"I have to talk to the Dragon Spirit," Aang explained. "He can help me defeat the Fire Nation. Is there a spiritual place where I can meditate?"

Princess Yue nodded. "There is a very spiritual place here," she said. "The city was built around it. Come. We must hurry."

The princess led Aang, with Momo riding on his shoulder, Sokka, and Katara through the city. They passed waves of panicked people racing through the streets, alarmed about the arrival of the Fire Nation at their shore. In the section of the city farthest from the ocean, the buildings gave way to a sheer, ice-covered mountain that formed the rear boundary of the Water Tribe stronghold.

"This way," Princess Yue told the others, leading them up a steep set of stairs that brought them to a passageway through the mountain. The corridor was lined with flaming torches. At the end of the passageway, the group came to a closed door.

"This is it," the princess said. "The entrance to the spiritual place." She opened the door slowly. It creaked as it swung on ancient hinges.

Stepping through the doorway, the group found themselves in a courtyard filled with lush green grass and tall trees. The area was completely surrounded on all sides by high walls of ice. It looked as if a small piece of a tropical paradise had been dropped down right in the middle of a frozen mountain.

"Wow, Katara, it's warm in here," Sokka cried, unbuttoning his heavy winter coat. "That is so weird. Just on the other side of that door, it's freezing."

"My father never told me why this place is sacred," Yue said, gazing up through the trees.

Momo flew from Aang's shoulder and landed at the edge of a koi pond that sat right in the center of the grassy oasis. The pond was fed by a stream that ran like a ribbon of water through the spiritual place. Aang followed the lemur-bat and sat beside him in the soft grass. A feeling of peace washed over him as he stared into the pond and watched two koi fish—one white with a black spot, the other black with a white spot—swim around inside it.

Momo reached out quickly and tried to grab one of the fish. It evaded his grasp.

"Momo, be nice," Aang scolded his pet. Momo grumbled and scampered away from the pond.

Aang leaned in closer to the water, fascinated by the movements of the two fish. He felt as if he could sit there and watch them all day. He stared as they circled around each other, forming a living circle in the still water, and felt his eyes begin to close.

His friends in turn stared at Aang, watching as he sat perfectly still.

"I have to get back," Princess Yue whispered so as not to disturb Aang's meditation. "My tribe needs me in this time of crisis."

Sokka nodded. "I'll take you," he whispered. "We have to be able to see what the Fire Nation warships are doing."

"I'll stay with Aang," Katara said softly.

Yue and Sokka slipped back through the door, which creaked again as they closed it behind them.

"Aang?" Katara whispered, leaning in close to his ear. "Aang, can you hear me?"

Aang said nothing. He remained perfectly still. His eyes stayed closed.

"I knew you were real," Katara said, fingering her necklace as her eyes welled up with tears. "I always knew you'd return."

Katara took a deep breath and regained her composure. She turned suddenly at the sound of the entry door creaking, expecting to see Sokka or Yue. Instead she watched in horror as Prince Zuko entered the spiritual place. In his hand he clutched a flaming torch he had taken from the passageway.

"I always knew he would return too," Zuko said, closing the door behind him and staring hard at Katara.

"The Fire Lord's son!" Katara cried. "You took him from our village. Aang said you tried to take him from the Fire Nation at the Northern Air Temple. I won't let you take him from here."

Zuko dropped the torch, setting the grass on fire. He stepped forward with a firebending move that sent a burst of flames tearing toward Katara. She stood her ground, as Master Pakku had taught her, and drew a torrent of water from the nearby stream with a waterbending move. Water and fire met in midair, forming a harmless column of steam.

Zuko stepped forward again, repeating his firebending move. But again, Katara met his blast with a stream of water that extinguished the flames.

"Who are you?" Zuko asked, unable to hide that he was impressed by this girl's ability as a bender.

"My name is Katara, and I'm the only waterbender left in the Southern Water Tribe," Katara said proudly, unafraid of the Fire Lord's son.

Zuko spun into an advanced firebending move, his arms and legs moving in a blur. Flames shot up from the burning grass into two fiery arcs heading for Katara from opposite directions. Stunned for a moment by the size and complexity of Zuko's attack, Katara pulled a jet of water from the stream. The water struck one of the fire arcs, putting it out, but the second arc blasted into her. She slumped to the ground, unconscious.

Zuko stood over Katara's singed, motionless form, staring. Then he looked up at Aang, who had not moved from the edge of the koi pond during the battle.

"I'm not allowed to go home without him," Zuko said, as if explaining his actions to the unconscious Katara. Then he threw Aang over his shoulder and hurried from the spiritual place.

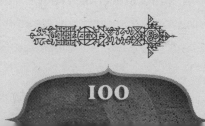

In the stronghold's main courtyard, spinning drills broke through the icy ground in dozens of spots, opening holes. Black-clad Fire Nation soldiers emerged from the sea below, crawling out onto the ground, then scrambling to their feet.

Alarms blared and the crowd of terrified Water Tribe villagers ran from the courtyard, scattering into the city. At the same time, the Fire Nation ships just outside the stronghold wall launched flaming metal cages filled with fire over the wall and into the city.

A huge metal platform lowered from the lead Fire Nation ship and landed on the top of the wall. Firebenders riding enormous creatures, half rhino and half Komodo dragon, charged from the ship, up the platform, onto the wall, and into the city. Bending the fire from the flaming metal cages, the firebenders atop the massive beasts sent blazing streams of destruction down onto the city.

The Fire Nation invasion of the Northern Water Tribe stronghold, the Fire Lord's best hope for ending the growing rebellion against him, was now fully underway.

Appa soared through the sky, carrying Sokka and Princess Yue on his back. Now that the fight had begun, they desperately needed the Avatar.

"There it is, Appa!" Sokka cried as they cleared the outer wall of the spiritual place. "That's where we need to land."

The sky bison drifted down into the spiritual place and landed on the scorched grass. Sokka and Yue jumped from his back and ran toward the koi pond.

"Katara, Aang, the Fire Nation is in the city!" Sokka cried. "We need you guys."

Princess Yue looked all around. "Where's the Avatar?" she asked.

That's when Sokka spotted the unconscious form of his sister, stretched out on the charred ground. "Katara!" he shouted in fear, quickly running to her side. He gently lifted Katara into a sitting position and leaned her against a tree. She moaned, then winced in pain as her eyes slowly opened.

"Are you all right?" Sokka asked, relieved to see his sister stirring. "What happened?"

Katara looked toward the koi pond. "Prince Zuko's here in the city. He took Aang again!"

CHAPTER 15

Aang's eyes opened slowly. He immediately realized that he was back in the spirit world. He was pleased that the power of the spiritual place had worked and allowed him to return here. But now he had to find the Dragon. He needed help. He ran through the spirit world forest, searching for the Dragon's cave.

The glow of lanterns just ahead cut through the thick mist.

"Hello," he called out, moving deeper into the darkness. Slamming into what he thought was a wall, Aang stopped short when he noticed the Dragon's opened eyes. The harsh sound of dragon scales scraping against the walls filled the cave.

"Please tell me how to beat the Fire Nation," Aang pleaded with the Dragon, staring into the beast's enormous eyes.

"You must show them the power of Water," the Dragon said in a booming voice that echoed around the cave. The creature brought its mammoth head right up to Aang's face, pinning the young Avatar against a cave wall. "They have forgotten that all the elements are equal. That is why an Avatar must exist—to prove by your example that this is true."

Aang grew concerned. "Do I have to hurt the Fire Nation soldiers?" he asked. The monks who raised him had taught Aang that all life was precious and that the great power he commanded should only be used defensively.

"You may have to hurt them," the Dragon replied.

As Aang pondered this, the Dragon slithered past him and slipped out of the cave.

"You spoke about my friends before," Aang called out to the Dragon. "You said there was some struggle. What were you trying to tell me?"

The Dragon turned around and peered back into the cave. "At some point you will have to make a difficult choice," the Dragon explained. "Between Katara and being the Avatar."

Before Aang could reply, the Dragon spread its mighty wings and lifted itself into the sky. The gust of the wind created by the flapping wings sent a rush of mist into the cave that engulfed Aang.

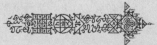

Prince Zuko sat against the wall of a storage room in the stronghold. Seated next to him, leaning against a wall, was

Aang, unconscious, his hands bound together with rope. His breathing was steady, his eyes moving constantly behind his closed eyelids.

Peering through a window in the room, Zuko saw crowds of panicked people, running. He heard the sounds of battle just beyond the tiny room.

"We'll just wait until everyone's fighting everyone," Zuko said softly to the sleeping boy beside him. "Then in the night, we'll slip out."

He stared at Aang for a few moments more, then continued talking. "That must be some dream you're having," he said, pausing to think about the fact that the Avatar was finally in his grasp. "I have to bring you back to my father. He'll be proud. He's never been proud of me. My sister, Azula, was always the special one. She was a firebending prodigy. My father loves her, but he can't even look at me. He says I'm like my mother."

Zuko's speech was interrupted by the sound of Aang, scrambling to his feet.

"You're awake," Zuko cried, standing up quickly, just as Aang slipped behind a group of barrels. "Don't move, Airbender!"

Aang jumped up onto a barrel and kicked off into the air. Zuko drew fire from a torch in the room and aimed it in the direction that Aang had gone. The flames narrowly missed him.

Turning to bend fire from another torch, Zuko lost sight

of his prey. He lit every corner of the room, searching. Sensing movement behind him, Zuko spun and sent a wave of fire toward the door where Aang had silently moved. A cluster of barrels near the door burst into flames, blocking Aang's escape route.

"Got you!" Zuko cried, flinging a massive stream of fire at Aang.

Aang used airbending to create a spinning shield of wind, which sent the fire spurting off in all directions. But Zuko kept up his relentless attack.

Suddenly the room began to rumble. A group of barrels in the center of the room began to shake. Zuko spun toward the middle of the room, just as water shot out from six of the barrels, like long arms. The water wrapped all around Zuko, then instantly froze, trapping him in a solid block of ice. He was completely covered, except for a small bubble of air around his head.

Aang turned toward the doorway in time to see Katara complete a waterbending move. She rushed into the room, follow by Sokka and Yue.

"Are you okay?" Katara asked Aang, throwing her arms around him.

He nodded.

"Did the spirits tell you anything?" Katara asked as she untied Aang's hands.

"Yes," he replied with a frown. "But I'm still not sure what to do."

"Let's go," Katara said, running from the room, followed closely by Sokka and Yue. Aang lingered for a moment. He stepped toward Zuko, bringing his hands to his waist in a waterbending move that melted the ice all around Zuko's head.

The Fire Nation prince coughed and gasped for breath. He shivered from the cold.

"You won't be killed by waterbenders if you stay hidden here," Aang said as he dashed to the door. Just before he left the room, he turned back to Zuko and added, "It was fun escaping with you from the Air temple. We could be friends, you know." Then he turned and ran from the room to join his friends.

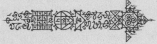

Commander Zhao stood on the deck of his warship with Iroh beside him. They watched as Fire Nation war machines tore gaping holes in the stronghold's outer wall. Fire Nation soldiers and firebenders continued to pour into the city.

"I advise that you pull back your men soon," Iroh said, glancing up at the late afternoon sun. "They will be trapped in the city when the moon's power comes out and strengthens the waterbenders."

"Do not be worried about the moon's power, General Iroh," Zhao said without moving.

Iroh stepped back in surprise. "Why should we not be worried about the moon's power?" he asked anxiously.

"Because your brother, Fire Lord Ozai, and I have

decided it's in our best interests to kill the Moon Spirit," Zhao replied.

"What?" Iroh cried, horrified by the idea. He turned and went below to his quarters.

As evening descended a short while later, Zhao and Iroh left the ship and entered the Water Tribe stronghold, flanked by Fire Nation soldiers.

"They're getting stronger as night comes on," Zhao said, watching the fierce fighting all around him. He pulled out a scroll. "This is from the Great Library. It is our map. I know exactly where we need to go."

Zhao turned to his men. "Our world is going to change soon, gentlemen," he announced over the sounds of battle. "Follow me."

Spotting a group of Fire Nation soldiers surrounding a uniformed man holding a tattered scroll, Aang and his friends paused.

"You guys follow them," Aang suggested. "I'm going to join the fight in the main courtyard."

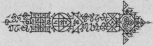

Katara, Sokka, and Yue followed Commander Zhao and his soldiers as Aang dashed off to the courtyard. Stepping right into the battle, Aang used waterbending to create a cage of ice around a Fire Nation soldier. Moving forward, Aang whipped his hands to the right, causing a circle of ice to plummet ten feet, sending another soldier plunging into a pit.

In a reverse move, Aang lifted a huge column of ice right under a soldier who found himself suspended high above the fray. Aang trapped another soldier inside a ball of ice that rolled harmlessly away from the battle.

As Aang continued to fight, Zhao, Iroh, and the soldiers followed the scroll, which led them right to the spiritual place. Pushing open the creaky door, the uninvited guests stepped in.

Zhao walked to the pond and looked down at the two fish circling each other as they had always done. "They are called many names," Zhao said. "Ying and Yang. Push and Pull."

Iroh joined Zhao at the edge of the pond.

"General Iroh, may I introduce you to the mysterious Ocean and Moon Spirits," Zhao said.

Iroh stared down at the fish in wide-eyed amazement.

Zhao pulled out a pouch, which he proceeded to dip into the pond. With a scooping motion, he caught the white fish inside it. Lifting the pouch from the water, he tied it shut, clutching the squiggling, squirming bag firmly in his grip.

"Why do spirits take the form of such benign things?" Zhao asked as the bag in his hand shook more furiously. "It leaves them so vulnerable."

"To teach man kindness and humility," Iroh replied, filled with horror as the true nature of Zhao's plan became clear. He glanced up at the moon, which grew dimmer as the Moon Spirit struggled for breath, trapped within Zhao's pouch.

"Commander Zhao, there are certain things humankind should not tamper with," Iroh cried, unable to hold his tongue any longer. "The spirit world is one of those things."

Zhao looked at Iroh with contempt. "That's what we teach to our children, isn't it?" he snarled.

Just then, Katara, Sokka, and Yue burst through the door of the spiritual place.

"What are you doing here?" Katara shouted at Zhao. He said nothing, but simply lifted up the bag in his hand. The Moon Spirit flopped around beneath his firm grasp.

"What's he holding?" Katara asked Yue.

"I think he has one of the fish from the pond," Yue said. "My father said never to touch those fish."

"I am holding your Moon Spirit, Princess," Zhao stated, balling his free hand into a fist and drawing it back, never taking his eyes off the bag in his other hand.

"Stop, Zhao!" Iroh shouted. "The world will go out of balance. Everyone will be hurt."

Zhao looked at Iroh and smirked. "The Fire Nation has become too powerful to worry about children's superstitions, General Iroh," Zhao said with a sneer.

At their feet, the black Ocean Spirit fish swam frantically, sensing that its partner, its balance, had been disturbed.

"Commander Zhao, don't!" Iroh yelled.

"We have no need of gods," Zhao said, his voice choked with emotion. "*We* are now gods!"

"No," Iroh said sadly. "We have gone too far."

A twisted smile spread across Zhao's face. He punched the pouch with a mighty blow.

It stopped moving, and Princess Yue collapsed onto the grass, as if she were the one who had been punched.

CHAPTER 16

In the courtyard, Aang battled fiercely, waterbending ice prisons, shields, platforms, and pits, trapping and stopping Fire Nation soldiers.

Above him the brilliant white moon flickered and grew steadily dimmer. Pain shot through his head, as if he had been struck. The moon slowly turned fire red, casting a sickly crimson glow over the entire Water Tribe stronghold.

Aang clutched his head, feeling completely disoriented. The waterbenders around him stumbled aimlessly, lost and confused, as more Fire Nation soldiers poured through the outer wall and rushed into the courtyard.

Back in the spiritual place, Zhao opened his pouch and dumped out the lifeless fish. It splashed into the pond and floated on its side.

Iroh's eyes filled with tears as rage built up inside him.

"You are too soft, General Iroh," Zhao snarled. "You are too blind to see that this is the future."

Staring at Zhao, Iroh's eyes grew dark and wide. He began breathing slowly and deeply, then suddenly thrust his hands toward the sky. To everyone's amazement, fire shot from his hands, forming huge arcs of flame.

The Fire Nation soldiers drew back, stunned and frightened.

"He is creating fire out of nothing!" cried one of the soldiers. They all ran in fear.

Firebenders had the ability to control and manipulate fire. But they were not supposed to be able to create fire where there was none.

Commander Zhao, unable to comprehend this great power—and certainly unable to combat it—turned and fled from the spiritual place, along with his men.

Iroh lowered his hands, and the flames died down, then disappeared. The exhausted firebender knelt by the pond and sadly watched as the frantic Ocean Spirit fish swam around and around the floating body of its Moon Spirit companion.

Sokka helped Princess Yue to her feet and over to the pond.

In a weak voice, barely loud enough to be heard, she whispered, "All is now lost."

Iroh looked at Yue. Spotting her pure white hair, his

expression changed from despair to curiosity. "You have been anointed by the Moon Spirit?" he asked the princess.

"He gave me life when I was a child," she replied faintly.

"Then there is still a chance," Iroh said with hope, gently taking Yue's hand. "You can give your life back for the spirit's."

"What!" Sokka cried, turning to Iroh. "What are you talking about, old man?" He turned back to Yue. "He's Fire Nation. Don't listen to him."

"Nothing is ever truly lost," Iroh said softly.

Princess Yue stared at the Fire Nation general. His face was worn, but kindly. And he had objected to the horrible actions of the commander. Somehow, she trusted him instinctively. "Is my life mine to give back if I choose?" she asked.

"There are reasons each of us is born," Iroh replied. "We have to find those reasons."

Yue turned her head in the direction of the battle raging just beyond the ice walls. She listened to the helpless sounds of the waterbenders of her tribe, their bending ability now gone. "This is the reason I was born," she stated with certainty.

Sokka reached out and took Yue by the arm. He had never felt about anyone the way he felt about Yue, and he could not bear the thought of losing her now. "Yue, please," he pleaded, his eyes filling with tears. "You have to lead your people."

The princess leaned close and whispered into Sokka's

ear. "That is what I am doing. There is no love without sacrifice. My father taught me that."

Sokka held her tightly. Then Princess Yue stepped into the pond. The water began to glow white, and as the water grew brighter, Yue's hair transitioned from white to black.

The glowing stopped, and the Moon Spirit fish began swimming in unison with the Ocean Spirit, its life restored. Princess Yue's limp body collapsed into the pond. Sokka and Iroh gently pulled her wet, lifeless body out of the water and placed her on the soft grass.

Sokka leaned over Yue's body and wept for his best friend.

Back in the courtyard, Aang looked up to see the red glow of the moon fade, replaced by its usual bright, white brilliance. He and the tribe's waterbenders felt their power renewed and their spirits lifted. They rejoined the battle with newfound energy.

On a nearby bridge Commander Zhao watched in disgust as the moon regained its normal appearance. A figure appeared at the far end of the bridge, blocking his way.

Zhao stared in disbelief at Prince Zuko. "I killed you!" he cried. "I blew up your ship."

Iroh suddenly ran up to his nephew as four waterbenders approached Zhao. "Come away from him, nephew!" Iroh shouted. "There are too many soldiers and waterbenders here now. They will never let you take the Avatar. We must leave immediately."

Zuko stood his ground, staring at Zhao with deadly intensity.

"He wants to fight you so he can capture you," Iroh called out to Zuko. "Just walk away."

Zuko understood the wisdom of his uncle's words. If he fought Zhao here, he might never get the chance to capture the Avatar. Retreating for the moment and coming up with a new strategy was the better choice. He turned and walked off the bridge.

At that moment Zhao directed a blast of fire from some burning debris right at Zuko's back. Iroh stepped forward quickly, placing himself between the flames and his nephew. Putting his palms together and extending his arms in front of him, Iroh formed a spear shape and redirected the flames, shielding Zuko.

"You stand alone," Iroh called out to Zhao when the flames had safely passed. "And that has always been your greatest mistake." Then the great Fire Nation general and his nephew hurried from the bridge.

As Zhao turned to leave, he found his path blocked by four waterbenders.

"There's nothing you can do," Zhao said, the contempt showing in his voice. "I already won this battle for the Fire Nation. They will always remember my name."

The four waterbenders said nothing. Instead, they lifted their hands and pulled four streams of water from the river that flowed beneath the bridge. The water surrounded and engulfed Zhao. Within seconds he could no longer breathe.

The waterbenders lifted Zhao, still encased in his watery prison, high above the bridge, where the Fire Nation commander drowned in midair. Releasing their hold, the waterbenders allowed Zhao to come crashing down, his body sprawled out in the spreading puddle. Then they turned and ran back to the battle still raging in the courtyard.

Back at that battle, Sokka looked across the courtyard in horror to see the outer wall breaking open, allowing a new squadron of Fire Nation soldiers to rush through.

"Katara," he cried out. "They broke through!"

"Keep fighting!" Katara shouted back as she battled beside her fellow waterbenders.

"There's so many," Aang called out, beginning to lose hope.

Within moments the waterbenders, so greatly outnumbered, were overwhelmed. Master Pakku fought fiercely, but eventually he grew exhausted. Even with Aang fighting at their side, the city seemed lost, and with it, any chance of stopping the Fire Nation's plan for world domination.

"Don't let Yue have died in vain," Sokka pleaded.

Aang's mind flashed back not to the spirit world, but

to the words of Master Pakku. "Water is the element of change," Master Pakku's voice sounded in his head. "You must let your emotions flow like water."

In an instant Aang knew what he had to do. He spun his body and rotated his hands, sending an airbending blast through the courtyard. The powerful wind pushed open a path through the battle forces, leading right to the city's outer wall.

"Do it for Yue!" Sokka shouted.

Aang raced to the wall and bounded up the stairs. Within seconds he stood at the top, looking out at the vast Fire Nation fleet in the ocean just beyond.

Again, Master Pakku's voice filled his mind. "Flow like water."

Aang's vision blurred as he saw images from his own life flashed before him: walking with Monk Gyatso at the Southern Air Temple, learning airbending, reading the ancient scrolls, praying with the monks, and playing with his friends.

Then, all of a sudden he was the Avatar. Now all of those friends and teachers were gone, killed by the Fire Nation. And now that same nation was threatening to destroy another tribe. Not this time. This time he would be the Avatar.

The ocean and the Fire Nation ships came back into his view through tear-filled eyes. Taking a deep breath, he let his emotions flow, just like water. Using every bit of his waterbending skill, Aang lifted his hands into graceful arcs, again and again.

At first the ocean rose slightly, obeying Aang's waterbending commands but still moving under its own force. Aang again lifted his hands. This time the ocean rose higher. Encouraged by his success, Aang felt his confidence grow, which in turn increased his power.

He could feel the mighty force of the water obeying his command, and raised his hands high above his head. The ocean responded by roaring into the sky, and then plummeted to crash against the sea wall that protected the city.

Like a giant hand swatting insects, the ocean reached up and swept away the latest group of soldiers trying to enter the city from their ships. As the water rose higher, Aang's movements grew faster and smoother, as if he had been waterbending his entire life. His tattoos began to glow furiously as he claimed his rightful role as great peacekeeper of the world.

Down in the courtyard, the Fire Nation soldiers stopped fighting and looked up in horror at the sight of the ocean curling above the wall. Panicked, they ran to escape from the city, but there was nowhere to run. Those who made it out of the city got swept up by the raging sea. Those who stayed simply surrendered, realizing they had no chance for escape—or victory.

Back on the wall, Aang felt a comforting combination

of incredible power and absolute calm pulsing through his body. His movements became more and more focused as the sea he now controlled changed direction and roared out toward the great Fire Nation fleet.

Sokka and Katara looked up and watched Aang in amazement as the ocean towered above him, reaching into the sky. As the water curled back into the ocean, it crashed down onto the Fire Nation fleet.

Onboard the ships, captains shouted orders, commanding powerful engines be reversed. Massive waves curled up around them. Many ships vanished beneath the powerful churning and swirling of the water.

What was left of the once-invincible fleet turned and retreated. Some of those ships were overcome by the force of the waves. The ones that did escape, quickly disappeared from view. Aang had succeeded. The Fire Nation army had been turned away.

Already out on the ocean, some distance from the massive tidal wave that swamped the Fire Nation fleet, Zuko and Iroh paddled swiftly in a stolen Water Tribe kayak.

Looking back, Iroh turned to his nephew in awe. "The Avatar has mastered Water."

Zuko kept paddling, saying nothing.

Katara dashed up the steps that led to the top of the wall in time to see Aang lower his hands. The ocean returned to normal, gently lapping against the stronghold's base.

"Aang?" she asked tentatively. "Are you all right?"

He turned to her and nodded, although she could see he was weak from the enormous effort battling the Fire Nation. She wrapped an arm around Aang and led him to the staircase, where they met Sokka running up the stairs.

Aang draped one arm across the shoulder of each of his friends, and they helped him down the stairs. Stepping out into the courtyard, Aang saw the entire Northern Water Tribe waiting for him. Moving as one, they all knelt down and bowed before him. The remaining Fire Nation soldiers who had not gotten out of the city also bowed.

"They want you to be their Avatar, Aang," Katara said, smiling at her friend. "We all do."

Aang hesitated for a moment, recalling again the moment he first discovered he was the Avatar—when all his friends and teachers bowed to him. He didn't feel worthy then, and he worried that he was not completely worthy now. Although he was proud his waterbending skills helped save the Northern Water Tribe, he still couldn't bend two of the elements. How long would those take to master? Would he be able to bend earth and fire before the comet came again? Would he be able to save the people of the four nations again? Aang still had so many questions, but he knew he was on the right path. So, he stepped forward, pulling away from Sokka and Katara. His friends joined the others and bowed to their Avatar. Aang put his hands together and bowed back to everyone.

He knew his destiny was sealed. He knew who he truly was.

The Last Airbender, and the one true Avatar.

EPILOGUE

In the field in front of the Fire Lord's palace, a young soldier cautiously approached Fire Lord Ozai.

"My lord, our forces at the Northern Water Tribe have failed," he reported. "Commander Zhao was killed."

The Fire Lord stared silently at the young soldier.

"There is good news," the soldier continued. "Your son was seen alive with General Iroh. No one knows where they went. And there is something else, my lord. General Iroh displayed the ability to self-manifest fire during the battle."

Still the Fire Lord said nothing.

The soldier continued. "And the Avatar . . . they said the Avatar can bend three fields of water. They say he can bend the ocean."

Still saying nothing, Fire Lord Ozai moved his hand, firebending embers from a burning stick of incense onto the edge of the field. The grass instantly caught fire and began to spread rapidly.

"When this fire has reached three fields in length, I want you to try and stop it," the Fire Lord said. Then he turned and walked slowly back to his palace.

The young soldier, frightened and confused, watched as the fire spread three fields in length . . . and beyond.

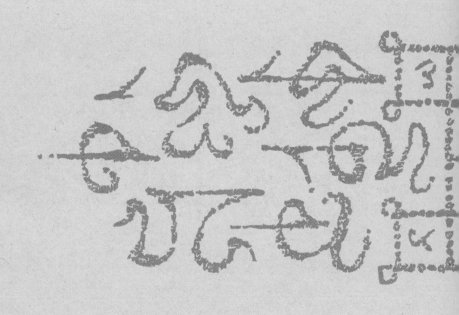

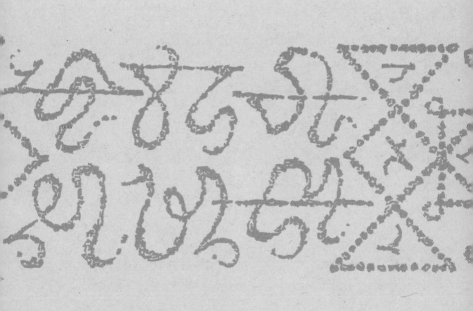